COUNTRY LEGACY

SHIPMENT 1

Courted by the Cowboy by Sasha Summers
A Valentine for the Cowboy by Rebecca Winters
The Maverick's Bridal Bargain by Christy Jeffries
A Baby for the Deputy by Cathy McDavid
Safe in the Lawman's Arms by Patricia Johns
The Rancher and the Baby by Marie Ferrarella

SHIPMENT 2

Cowboy Doctor by Rebecca Winters
Rodeo Rancher by Mary Sullivan
The Cowboy Takes a Wife by Trish Milburn
A Baby for the Sheriff by Mary Leo
The Kentucky Cowboy's Baby by Heidi Hormel
Her Cowboy Lawman by Pamela Britton

SHIPMENT 3

A Texas Soldier's Family by Cathy Gillen Thacker
A Baby on His Doorstep by Roz Denny Fox
The Rancher's Surprise Baby by Trish Milburn
A Cowboy to Call Daddy by Sasha Summers
Made for the Rancher by Rebecca Winters
The Rancher's Baby Proposal by Barbara White Daille
The Cowboy and the Baby by Marie Ferrarella

SHIPMENT 4

Her Stubborn Cowboy by Patricia Johns
Texas Lullaby by Tina Leonard
The Texan's Little Secret by Barbara White Daille
The Texan's Surprise Son by Cathy McDavid
It Happened One Wedding Night by Karen Rose Smith
The Cowboy's Convenient Bride by Donna Alward

COUNTRY
LEGACY

THE MAVERICK'S RETURN

USA TODAY BESTSELLING AUTHOR

Marie Ferrarella

Special thanks and acknowledgment are given to
Marie Ferrarella for her contribution to the
Montana Mavericks: The Great Family Roundup continuity.

Recycling programs
for this product may
not exist in your area.

ISBN-13: 978-1-335-52353-2

The Maverick's Return
First published in 2017. This edition published in 2022.
Copyright © 2017 by Harlequin Enterprises ULC

For questions and comments about the quality of this book,
please contact us at CustomerService@Harlequin.com.

Harlequin Enterprises ULC
22 Adelaide St. West, 41st Floor
Toronto, Ontario M5H 4E3, Canada
www.Harlequin.com

Printed in U.S.A.

To
Marcia Book Adirim,
Whose multilevel mind
Always leaves me in complete
Awe

Prologue

Daniel Stockton wearily walked into the log cabin he lived in at the Comanchero Ranch. For the last ten years, he'd been in charge of booking vacations for city dwellers who yearned to sample the cowboy life for a week or two and pretend they lived back in the days of the old Wild West. The dude ranch, one of Colorado's most popular, was currently in the height of its busy season. Attendance was at an all-time high and would probably remain so until somewhere around the end of next month.

As he concentrated on putting one foot in front of the other on the way to his second-hand sofa, Dan felt as if all those years had been packed into this last week and a half.

He sighed and collapsed on the worn, cracked sofa in the center of his small living area.

His stomach rumbled, asking to be appeased, but for now, Dan felt as if he couldn't move more than the first two fingers of his right hand. The hand that was currently wrapped around the remote control for the TV that had been in the cabin when he'd initially moved in. The cabin was too quiet and he just wanted some background noise to distract him.

Even now, after all these years, he didn't like being alone with his thoughts.

Aiming the remote at the twenty-four-inch TV screen, he pressed the power button, content to watch whatever program came on. He just wanted some company he didn't have to explain anything to. The tourists who came to the ranch always seemed to be filled to the brim with questions.

Most of the time, that didn't bother him, but there was this one family this last week that had a kid with them—Harlan—who just wouldn't stop asking questions no matter what. The kid, all of eleven or twelve, was obviously trying to trip him up.

Dan felt as if his head was throbbing and, quite possibly, on the verge of exploding.

The pay at the Comanchero Ranch was fairly decent and he did get to spend most of his life on horseback, which he loved, but there were times—like this last week—when the loneliness caught up to him, wrapping its tentacles around him so hard he could scarcely breathe. That was when he found his patience to be thin and in relatively short supply. And when that happened, his tolerance went out the window.

This afternoon he'd come dangerously close to telling Harlan's parents that they needed to take their son in hand and teach him some much-needed manners. But he'd managed to hold his tongue long enough to get those "dudes" back to the ranch house where they were staying.

However, it had been close. Closer than he really liked.

"Get a grip, Dan. This isn't a bad job. And you sure as hell can't afford to lose it," he told himself as he got up again.

His stomach was growling way too much.

It was time to rummage through his refrigerator and find something that could pass for food.

As he walked to the small refrigerator, his back was to the TV when he heard it.

The voice from his past.

Dan froze, listening. Convinced that he was imagining things.

It couldn't be, he told himself. It was the loneliness getting to him, wearing away his edge, nothing more.

He forced himself to proceed to the kitchen and open the refrigerator. Instead of getting something to eat, he took out a bottle of root beer, twisted off the cap and closed the refrigerator door.

He'd just put the bottle to his lips when he heard it again.

The voice from his past.

"This is Travis Dalton and you're watching *The Great Roundup.* We're coming to you live from Rust Creek Falls, Montana, and I'm here talking to Jamie Stockton, the valiant dad of year-old triplets. Jamie, until just recently, had to juggle being both father *and* mother to these fine, hearty little human beings. Tell us how that felt, Jamie."

"I don't mind admitting that I was pretty overwhelmed at first," the young man the narrator had addressed as Jamie answered.

The root beer slipped from Dan's hand, meeting the floor at an obtuse angle. Mercifully, it avoided shattering. Instead, a small shower of foam emerged from the bottle, christening his boots and the bottom of his jeans.

Dan didn't notice.

His eyes were glued to the TV, staring at the screen.

Staring at Jamie Stockton.

His younger brother.

The wave of loneliness Dan had been harboring turned into a twelve-foot sweeping tidal wave, all but drowning him in memories.

Memories he had been struggling so hard to bury and ignore for the last twelve years.

Listening to the voice of the young man telling his story caused those years to instantly melt away as if they had never happened.

Except that they had.

Chapter 1

Daniel shifted from foot to foot, standing before the closed ranch house door.

His brother's door.

He had absolutely no idea what to expect. What if, when his brother Jamie opened the door and saw who was knocking, he slammed it in his face?

Of course, there was a small chance, one that he was silently rooting for, that Jamie would mercifully allow him to plead his case.

The way he felt, however, the odds were probably against that happening.

It had taken Dan more than a whole month

of intense soul searching to finally get up the nerve to take this giant step, to leave Colorado and travel all this distance back to Rust Creek Falls, Montana.

Back to his hometown and his roots.

Back to the place where it had all fallen apart twelve years ago.

Ironically, the very things that were drawing him back to Rust Creek Falls were the same things that had caused him to stay away so long in the first place.

The same things that made him hesitate reconnecting this last whole month.

Dan had raised his hand to knock on the door a total of three times now. And all three times his courage had failed him, causing him to drop his hand back down again to his side.

Come on. You didn't come all this way back to Montana just to chicken out at the last minute. This isn't you.

Except that, maybe, it was. Why else had he not tried to get back in contact with *any* of his siblings for over a decade?

The first two years of his self-imposed exile he'd been with his two older brothers, Luke and Bailey. But then they had gone their own separate ways, too, leaving him to fend for himself.

The simple truth of it was he was tired of being alone. Tired of having no one who shared at least part of the same memories from his childhood and adolescence.

Tired of not having any family.

It would have been different if he'd never had any siblings. He had very nearly made his peace with that. After all, he really had no idea where any of his brothers or sisters were anymore.

But then he'd heard Jamie's voice on that broadcast last month and everything had changed.

Suddenly, he felt as if he was part of something again. He knew that at least Jamie was still back in Rust Creek Falls. All he had to do was reach out, reestablish that familial connection with his younger brother and just like that, he would have a family again.

It had sounded so easy when he had first thought of it. But now he wasn't so sure.

At least find out if he'll talk to you.

Taking a deep breath, Dan raised his hand again and this time, his knuckles finally made contact with the door, creating a rhythmic sound as he knocked.

He could feel his heart pounding as he stood there, waiting.

It was late afternoon, almost early evening. What if there was no one at home? What if Jamie and his triplets were away on vacation? After all, that could be a possibility, Dan thought.

Or what if Jamie *was* home, opened the door and then told him to go to hell?

Dan's breath caught in his throat, all but turning solid.

What if—?

Suddenly, there was no more time for speculation or waffling. No more time for hypothetical what-ifs. The door opened and an older, adult version of the boy he had left behind twelve years ago, the young man he'd seen more than a month ago on his TV, was standing in the doorway, looking at him.

For a moment, the expression on Jamie Stockton's face was blank. It was the kind of expression a person wore when they opened their door to someone they didn't recognize.

But then, in the next moment, a multitude of emotions washed over Jamie's face in quick succession, one after the other.

Like a man caught in a dream, Jamie stared at him. And then, finally, he asked hoarsely, "Daniel?"

Dan's lips quirked in a quick, nervous smile. "Yeah. It's me," he confirmed, still feeling incredibly uneasy and uncertain about this reunion that he had instigated.

And then Dan cleared his throat and forced himself to push on and say something further. "I would have called ahead first, but I didn't know how you would react to seeing me and I didn't want to take a chance on you turning—"

Dan didn't get a chance to finish his sentence. Whatever else he was going to say about his concerns regarding their first meeting in twelve years evaporated when Jamie pulled him into his arms and enfolded him in a giant bear hug.

"Oh my God, Danny. It really is you!" Jamie cried, holding on to him tightly, as if he was afraid that if he opened his arms, his older brother would suddenly just vanish.

When after a couple of minutes Jamie gave no sign of releasing him, Dan finally had to say, "Um, Jamie, I think you're crushing my ribs."

"Oh, right. Sorry." Jamie let his arms drop. He took a step back and looked at Dan. Disbelief highlighted his face as his eyes raked over every square inch of his older brother. "It's just that I never thought I'd see you again. Come in, come in," he urged, gesturing into his house even as he ushered Dan in and closed the door behind him.

"Is everything okay? Are you here for a visit? Are you staying?" And then Jamie stopped asking questions. He took a deep breath, as if trying to get hold of himself. "Sorry, I don't mean to overwhelm you. It's just that there are so many things I want to know."

Before Dan could say a single word in response, Jamie broke out in another huge smile. "Damn, but it's good to see you!" he cried, pulling Dan into another heartfelt, although slightly less rib-crushing, bear hug.

This time, he released Dan without being prompted. A long sigh escaped him as he took a step back again.

"You've lost weight," Jamie finally noted.

"I wasn't exactly fat to begin with," Dan

reminded his brother with a self-conscious laugh.

"No, you weren't. But I don't recall your face looking this gaunt before— Damn, it's so great to see you," Jamie exclaimed again. "I thought… Well, for a while, I thought—" Jamie waved his hand. "Never mind what I thought. You're alive and you're here and that's all that counts." He blinked back tears that threatened to spill out. "Sit down. Make yourself comfortable," he urged, gesturing toward the leather sofa in his living room.

Relieved, Dan sat down beside his brother. "This is quite a welcome," he told Jamie, then confessed the fear that had almost made him turn around and go home before Jamie even knew he was there. "I was afraid you'd be angry with me."

"You mean for leaving?"

Dan nodded, looking uncomfortable as well as embarrassed. "Yes."

"I was," Jamie admitted. "I was really angry for a while. Angry and bitter that you and Luke and Bailey had just picked up and left us. Left me," he emphasized because that was what had been at the heart of his initial anger. "But then I realized that it wasn't your fault. After Mom and Dad died in that car crash, Grandma and Grandpa didn't exactly make it easy for the three of you to stick around."

As his brother spoke, memories of his grandparents assailed Daniel. Reliving those harsh days, even now, was painful. But he needn't explain them to Jamie, he realized, when his brother continued.

"I didn't find out the truth till much later. That they'd made it quite clear that they might have to take in Bella and me—since they managed to get the other girls adopted—but the three of you who were eighteen or older could fend for yourselves somewhere else. They all but told you, Luke and Bailey to leave town, so you really had no choice but to go."

Daniel could remember the day so clearly, though it had happened twelve years ago.

"But I didn't know at the time that they had said that to you," Jamie said. "All I knew was that my parents were dead and my big brothers had abandoned me just when I felt that I needed them the most." Jamie shook his head, trying to block the painful feeling those memories aroused. "I was really angry at you for a long time."

Dan made no effort to attempt to deflect the blame. However, the way Jamie had welcomed him was not the greeting of a man who still held a grudge.

"But you're not anymore?" Dan asked, wanting to be perfectly clear just where they stood in relation to one another.

"No, I'm not," Jamie readily confirmed.

Relief swamped him. Dan knew he should just accept that and be happy. He was aware that he was pushing his luck, but he had to know. "What changed your mind?"

Jamie laughed. "Simple. I found out that life's too short to carry around all this anger and bitterness. And the triplets came into my life. Nothing like being responsible for three tiny, helpless souls to make you get over yourself—fast," Jamie emphasized. "Once I stopped being so angry about everything, I left myself open for the good stuff, like love," he told Dan with a wide grin. "And that's when I fell in love with Fallon O'Reilly. After that, my whole world changed for the better— and now I couldn't be happier."

As if suddenly hearing himself, Jamie stopped right in the middle of his narrative, embarrassed. "Hell, I'm sorry."

"About what?" Dan asked, confused.

"Well, I'm doing all the talking here."

Dan shook his head. "That's okay. I think it's great. I haven't heard your voice in so long," he told Jamie. "Just keep talking."

But Jamie was not about to get sidetracked again. He had questions for his older brother.

"No, first tell me what made you suddenly turn up on my doorstep now, after twelve long years." Fresh fears suddenly surfaced in his mind. "Did something happen?" he wanted to know. "Has something suddenly changed? You're not dying, are you?" he asked, alarmed.

"No, I'm not dying," Dan assured his brother. "What happened was that I was in my cabin—"

Jamie cut in, surprised. "You have a cabin?"

"Yes," Dan answered. He didn't want to get into all that right now. That was for later. "Long story," he said, waving it away.

Jamie was starved for any and all information concerning Dan, not to mention the rest of his family, except for his sister Bella, who was still in Rust Creek Falls, and other sister Dana, who had recently been found.

"Go ahead, I'm all ears," Jamie told him.

Dan wanted to tell him about this part first, because it was what led to his coming back to Rust Creek Falls and to his seeking out Jamie. "I'll tell you about that once I finish answering your first question."

"Sorry, I didn't mean to interrupt," Jamie said, then coaxed, "Go ahead, I'm listening."

"All right, then." Taking a breath, Dan began again. "I'd just put in an extra-hard day. Walking into my cabin, I turned on the TV for some company—"

"So you live alone?"

Alone.

Each time Dan heard it, the word burned more and more of a hole in his gut. "Yeah, I do."

"You never married?" Jamie asked.

Dan shook his head. "Nope."

How could he marry? His heart was not his to give to anyone. It was already spoken for—even if the woman who it belonged to had no use for it.

When he hesitated, Jamie apologized.

"Sorry, didn't mean to pry," he told Dan. "Go on. You walked in, turned on the TV for company and then what?"

When he heard Jamie summarize the

events he'd just told him, the words had this incredibly lonely ring to them. He knew he'd felt the same thing time and again, but he'd talked himself into living with it. He'd made himself believe that his life wasn't as soul-draining as it really was. But now he knew the truth. That he was exceedingly lonely— and that he had made the right decision in coming home.

At least for now.

"And then I heard this voice," Dan said, continuing with his narrative, "this voice that was filled with pride and love, talking about his triplets."

"Wait," Jamie said, stopping his brother. "You heard me on TV? You caught that program that Travis Dalton taped in town? You actually saw *The Great Roundup*?"

Dan smiled at the eager disbelief he heard in his brother's voice. "I did."

"But that segment was on more than a month ago."

Dan merely nodded and said, "I know."

"You've been here in Rust Creek Falls all this time?"

"No, I just got here," Dan corrected. He wanted his brother to understand that it had been his cold feet that had kept him from coming. "You're my first stop. Possibly my only stop because I don't know where everyone else is, or even if they're still in Montana."

But Jamie was still having a hard time making sense out of what he was hearing. The brother he remembered, the one he had idolized, had never been someone to drag his feet.

"I don't understand. If the show was on over a month ago, what took you so long to get here?"

Dan wasn't about to lie or make up excuses. "It took me a month to get up the nerve to come and see you. I wasn't sure if you'd even let me come in your front door, or if you'd take one look at me, slam the door in my face and tell me to go to hell."

Jamie stared at him, an incredulous smile widening on his lips.

"You were afraid *I'd* reject you?" he asked.

Dan nodded. "Something like that."

The idea was so outlandish it almost made Jamie laugh out loud. "You were afraid of your little brother?" he asked, unable to believe that Danny could be afraid of anyone, least of all *him*.

Dan made no attempt at excuses, or to brazen the situation out. He was long past that sort of thing as far as he was concerned.

"Yes," Dan admitted, "I was. Because, as far as you were concerned, Luke, Bailey and I had run out on you and the girls. Left you at the mercy of a couple of cranky grandparents, neither of whom was ever going to be up for grandparent of the year. Left you and never tried to get in contact with you," Dan concluded with a sigh.

For a moment, the stark, honest answer left Jamie speechless. And then he said, "Well, at least you're not trying to sugarcoat any of it, I'll give you that."

"I can't sugarcoat it," Dan admitted. "I want you to know that I wanted to see you and the girls, wanted to get in contact with you." He put a hand on his brother's shoulder, anchoring him with the sincere look in his eyes. "Not a day went by in those years when I didn't think about you."

Jamie believed him. But he still had questions. "So if you felt that way, why didn't you get in contact with any of us?"

"I didn't want to disrupt your lives any

more than they'd already been disrupted," Dan told him with sincerity.

"You wouldn't have disrupted them, you idiot," Jamie cried. "You would have only made them better."

Dan sighed again. "Yeah, well…" His voice trailed off. At the time, he'd been convinced he was doing the right thing.

And then, of course, there had been the guilt. That had all but paralyzed him. It had definitely kept him from returning.

Jamie took pity on him. "Water under the bridge," he told Dan. "Just water under the bridge. What really matters is that you're here now," he said, sounding genuinely happy. "Makes my suffering through the taping of that program worth all the agony," he added with a warm laugh. "Oh damn, where are my manners? Can I offer you something to eat or drink?"

"No, I'm fine," Dan told him. "Just seeing you again after all this time is all I need."

"Speaking of need," Jamie said, "I need you to fill me in."

"On what?"

"On what you've been doing these last twelve years," Jamie said.

Dan blew out a long breath. He knew he owed Jamie that much. Still, going over that ground would bring up memories he wanted left buried and undisturbed.

He looked at Jamie, wondering where to start. "That, my brother, is a tall order."

Chapter 2

"Well," Jamie said in response to the unreadable expression on his brother's face, "think of it as the price you have to pay if you want to get to meet your nephews and niece."

The triplets, Dan thought. He'd almost forgotten about them.

"Okay," he replied gamely, "if you're really serious."

Jamie managed to keep a straight face for approximately fifteen seconds, and then he finally broke down and laughed.

"I'm just curious about what you've been

doing, but if you don't want to talk about it," he said more soberly, "that's okay."

Dan appreciated that his brother wasn't pressuring him for information. The very fact that Jamie wasn't encouraged him to share.

"It's not that I don't want to talk about it, Jamie. I just don't want to put you to sleep." The smile on his face was a tad sheepish. "The last twelve years have been pretty boring."

The sadness Jamie saw in his brother's eyes told him that those years weren't boring so much as they might have left a scar on Dan's soul. Jamie found himself aching for his brother.

"Tell me when you're ready," Jamie said. "No pressure."

Dan was about to say something in response, but just then, a slender, willowy redhead with lively blue eyes and an infectious smile walked into the room, coming from the back of the house. She looked straight at him.

"I thought I heard you talking to someone," she said to Jamie.

Both Jamie and his brother rose to their feet in unison.

"Danny," Jamie said, putting his hand out

to the woman who had just crossed over to them, "I'd like you to meet the light of my life, my wife, Fallon." Affectionately wrapping his arm around her waist, Jamie continued the introduction. "Fallon, this is my older brother Danny."

Jamie expected a nod of acknowledgment from the pretty young woman. A smile at best. But he quickly discovered that Fallon was just like her husband. Rather than greeting him with a few pleasantries, she left the shelter of her husband's arm and went straight to him.

The young woman embraced him, giving him a warm hug that swirled straight into his heart.

"Danny! It's so wonderful to finally meet you," she cried enthusiastically. "Jamie's told me so much about you!"

Stunned, still caught up in Fallon's embrace, Dan looked over her shoulder at his brother. He'd thought that by now, Jamie would have thought of him as a distant memory—if that.

"Really?" he asked.

"Yes," Fallon replied. Releasing her brother-in-law, she stepped back next to her husband.

"Can't get to know the man without getting to know his family. Though I must admit it took a bit of work at first. Jamie wasn't much of a talker in the beginning," she confided. "I think he kind of felt overwhelmed, and under the circumstances, who could blame him?" she said, looking at Jamie fondly. "But once I got him going, he told me all about you and Luke and Bailey, as well as your sisters. Bella and Dana, of course, I got to know myself. You've all had a rough life," she readily acknowledged, "but it can only get better from here on in."

Before Dan could ask about either Bella or Dana, Jamie told him, "Bella's still in Rust Creek Falls. She's married now. And Dana came for a while late last year. Turns out she's living in Portland, Oregon with a nice family who had adopted her. No word on Liza yet, but we're still looking." He smiled broadly at Danny. "Bella and Dana will both be thrilled to know that you're actually alive."

The revelation stunned Dan. He stared at his brother. "You didn't think I was alive?" he asked Jamie incredulously.

"Well, I didn't hear from you for twelve years. The thought had crossed my mind,"

Jamie said. "Anyway, it was Fallon who encouraged me to start looking, not just for you but for all the lost sheep of our family," he said. He paused to press a kiss to his wife's temple. "I don't mind telling you that this woman saved my life."

Fallon put her hand on her husband's chest. "Now, don't get all melodramatic on your brother, Jamie," Fallon chided.

"No melodrama," Jamie responded. "Just the plain truth. I was in a really bad way after Paula died," he told Dan.

"Paula?" Dan asked. It occurred to him that he knew next to nothing about what Jamie had gone through in the last twelve years, just what he had gotten from the TV program.

A pang twisted his gut. He should have been here. Somehow, even though his grandparents had all but thrown him and his older brothers out, he should have found a way to be there for Jamie and his sisters. A way to get over his all-but-soul-crushing guilt, a way to keep them all together as a family.

"His first wife," Fallon interjected.

The fact that Jamie had been married to someone else first didn't seem to bother her, Dan observed. She seemed to take it all in stride. Jamie had really lucked out with Fallon, Dan thought. He was genuinely happy for his brother. At least one of them had found happiness, despite the fact that the odds had felt as if they were against all of them.

"The triplets were born prematurely," Jamie explained, continuing to fill his brother in. "Paula died shortly after that from complications caused by the C-section. For a long while, I felt it was all my fault."

Confused, Dan wondered how that could possibly be his brother's fault.

"Paula didn't want kids. I did." A semi-sad smile played on his lips. "I guess I missed the sounds of a big family."

Fallon took over her husband's narrative. It was clear that she didn't want him to dwell on what she felt were his unfounded feelings of guilt.

"The whole town pitched in to help Jamie out when Paula passed on. A bunch of us took turns volunteering to take care of the triplets so that he could regain his foothold."

"I wouldn't have made it without you," Jamie told her.

"Without us," Fallon corrected. "Like I said," she told Dan, "the whole town pitched in."

Deftly, Fallon changed the subject, asking Dan, "So, have you come back to Rust Creek Falls to stay?"

"Not to sound as pushy as this redhead," Jamie interjected, "but have you?"

Dan was still trying to make his mind up about that. "I'm not sure yet."

Fallon didn't hesitate. "Well, you're staying with us while Jamie helps you to make up your mind," she told Dan. Her tone, warm and friendly, left no room for argument.

Still, Dan felt he had to at least offer a protest. "I can't impose."

"Family never imposes," Jamie insisted. "End of discussion. You're staying," he said with finality. Then he got back to his initial question. "So where have you been all this time?"

That was simple enough to answer. "The last ten years I've been in Colorado."

"Colorado?" Jamie repeated. "I can't picture you in Colorado."

Dan understood where Jamie was coming from on that. Colorado brought up images of big cities and he was a country boy at heart.

"I've been booking dude ranch vacations for city dwellers who fancy themselves cowboys," Dan told his brother and Fallon. "It's not a bad living," he was quick to add. "And I get to spend most of my time on horseback."

"Now, *that* I can picture," Jamie told him. "You said you've been in Colorado for the last ten years, but you've been gone from Rust Creek Falls for twelve. Where did you go before then?"

"Cheyenne," Dan answered. "I worked as a ranch hand there—along with Luke and Bailey. But they didn't much care for it," he confessed with a sad smile. "They got restless and then, one night, they just took off." He paused, trying to deal with an unexpected wave of sadness that washed over him. Suppressing a sigh, he told Jamie, "I haven't seen them since."

Fallon leaned forward and put her hand up on her brother-in-law's shoulder. "We'll find them," she promised.

"Isn't she amazing?" Jamie asked him. There was pride in his eyes. "She just keeps spreading optimism wherever she goes, no matter what."

A light pink hue rose to Fallon's cheeks as she pointedly ignored her husband's compliment. Rerouting the conversation again, she asked Dan, "Would you like to meet our kids?"

He could think of nothing that he would like better. "I'd love to," Dan responded.

"Then come this way. You can come too, Jamie," she added playfully, as if it was an afterthought. "Now, brace yourself," she told Dan. "These are not your typical year-and-a-half-old babies. They could use Jared, Henry and Kate in caffeine commercials," she confided.

"By the way, Kate's the one with a bow on her head," Jamie told him as they walked to the bedroom that the triplets occupied when they were downstairs.

He explained that the official nursery was upstairs, but because they wanted the triplets near them as much as possible, they'd created a second room for the babies downstairs where they could take their naps.

"She had such short hair," Jamie explained, "everyone thought I had three sons. After a while, I got tired of telling them that Kate was a girl, so I put a bow on her to set them straight."

"Now her hair is finally growing in," Fallon told him as she led the way into the back room. "Which is a good thing, because she keeps pulling that bow off."

Dan couldn't hold back the smile when he stepped into the room and saw the triplets. The two boys were both on their feet, their chubby little fingers grabbing the side of their playpen and shaking it. Dan had a feeling that the playpen's life expectancy was in serious jeopardy of being severely shortened.

The third triplet was seated on her well-padded bottom, serenely playing with a floppy-eared stuffed bunny, seemingly totally oblivious to the commotion her brothers were creating.

Beaming with unabashed pride, Jamie introduced his triplets.

"Dan, I'd like you to meet Henry and Jared," he said, indicating the two standing boys. "And this little sweetheart is Kate. Kids," Jamie said to his triplets, "this is your uncle Danny. Can you say 'Hi' to him?" he prompted.

An uneven chorus of something that could be thought to pass for "Hi!" rose up following Jamie's request.

"They talk?" Dan asked, his voice a mixture of surprise and envy. He knew next to nothing when it came to children and even less than that when it came to babies.

"Talk?" Jamie echoed, then said with a laugh, "They don't stop talking. Not even in their sleep. Of course, most of the time it sounds like gibberish and I can't understand what they're saying, but they seem to be able to communicate with each other just fine."

"That's because twins and triplets have a language all their own," Fallon told her husband.

Dan dropped to his knees beside the playpen to get closer to the three little people who had been instrumental in getting him to finally come home. Something stirred within him as he watched them for a moment.

"Hi, kids."

Again he received an uneven chorus echoing the greeting. Kate pulled herself up to her feet and made her way over to him. She offered him a sunny smile and just like that, she took him prisoner.

Dan ran his hand along her silky hair. "She's going to be a charmer," he told Jamie.

"What do you mean 'going to be'?" Jamie asked. "She already is one."

"You're right," Dan laughed, unable to take his eyes off the little girl. "My mistake."

Dan spent the next hour getting to know his brother's children as well as his brother's wife. It was the best hour he could remember spending in the last twelve years.

But then it was time to put the triplets down for a nap.

"I'm afraid you're going to have to leave the room now," Fallon told him, apologizing. "I'll never get them down for their naps if you're in eyesight."

"I understand," Dan said. He was already at the bedroom door, although he did pause for one last backward glance.

"They're something else, aren't they?" Jamie said with pride.

"They're beautiful kids," Dan agreed. And then he thought of the circumstances that Jamie had been forced to go through shortly after the triplets' birth. "You must have had a really hard time coping right after Paula's death," Dan said with immense sympathy. Again, he fervently wished he could have been there for Jamie.

"It was hard," Jamie admitted. "But Fallon wasn't kidding. It felt like the whole town pitched in to help. Otherwise, quite honestly, I don't know what would have happened or what I would have done. When you have just two hands and three kids, the numbers aren't exactly in your favor," he told his brother, his words underscored with a good-natured laugh.

Dan had been under the impression that Fallon had really meant a few people at best. But there was no reason for Jamie to exaggerate. That hadn't been in the nature of the boy he'd known.

"The *whole* town?" Dan asked in amazement, just to be sure.

"Yeah, the whole town." Jamie paused for a moment before adding, "Anne helped, too."

The mere mention of her name was like a fissure in the dam. The crack split open, spewing forth a deluge of memories upon Daniel.

"Have you been by to see Anne since you got back?" Jamie asked, breaking into his thoughts.

Not a day had gone by in the last twelve years that Dan hadn't wanted to see Anne Lattimore. That he hadn't wanted to pack up his meager belongings and find Annie. But he had staunchly never given in to that desire.

Mainly because he was convinced that she was far better off without him.

And even now, as he stood in his brother's house, battling the urge to ride up and see the woman he had loved practically from the first moment he'd drawn breath, a part of him still felt that she would be better off if he just left well enough alone.

"No," Dan answered quietly, "I haven't. When I came into town, I didn't stop anywhere else. I came straight to your place."

"I appreciate that, I really do," Jamie told him. "But if you ask me, I think that you really should go see her."

Jamie was tempted to say more, but he stopped himself. He pressed his lips together, as if physically blocking the words that had risen to his tongue.

"Maybe later," Dan demurred.

"There's already been too much 'later,' Danny. Twelve years of 'later.' You need to go see her. Now. Before any more time is lost. You can't get that time back. And the more you drag your feet, the more time you lose," Jamie insisted.

"When did you get this philosophical bent?" Dan asked, amused.

"Right about the time that I realized that I'd been in love with Fallon for a long time and needed to make her aware of it. Now, no more talk. It's still early. Go!" He opened the front door and all but pushed his brother out. "And when you've seen Anne and talked to her," he told Dan, "you can come back here—to your home."

Chapter 3

She missed him.

After all this time, she still missed him. Not every minute of every day the way she once had. Sometimes, Anne Lattimore could go a whole week without feeling that awful, painful hollowness boring a gaping hole into the pit of her stomach and working its way out to her soul. And then, suddenly, without giving her any warning, the feeling would be back, descending on her with its full weight, making her ache.

Making her remember.

And then she would have to struggle to

fight her way back out of the oppressive pit. Back into the light of day. Back into her life as a single mother and a full-time reception- ist at Dr. Brooks Smith's Veterinary Clinic.

Heaven knew there was enough in her life to keep her busy and most of the time, she was. Very busy. It was only during those eve- nings when Hank, her ex, would pick up Janie to have her stay overnight with him and the house was extra quiet that her mind would unearth images of Danny Stockton. That was when she would feel tormented.

Tormented, because even now she couldn't make peace with the fact that he had left town without saying anything.

Left *her* without saying anything.

After everything they had meant to one another...

No, Anne upbraided herself, she had only *thought* that they had meant so much to one another. Obviously, she hadn't meant to Danny nearly as much as he had meant to her.

She knew all the facts by now, having fer- reted them out over the years. She knew that Danny's grandparents had refused to be re- sponsible for him and his older brothers. Knew that they had all but *told* him and his brothers to leave. But if she had meant something to him, if Danny had loved her the way she loved him, he would have found a way to stay.

And if he couldn't abide staying in Rust Creek Falls, if he wanted to go somewhere else, she would have gone anywhere in the world with him. All he would have had to do was say that he wanted her to come with him and she would have left in a heartbeat. Left town, left her family, left her dreams of going to college. Left it all for Danny.

All he would have had to do was ask.

But he didn't ask.

Instead, he just disappeared without a trace, like some magician's big trick.

Even so, her pride badly wounded, she'd still tried to find him. But no one knew where Danny and his two brothers had gone. It was like they had vanished into thin air. Eventually, she gave up trying to find him, decided to go on with her life and went off to college.

And then Hank Harlow had happened in her life. It wasn't long after they met that Hank, clearly smitten, asked her to marry him. Ten years her senior, Hank wouldn't allow the age difference to get in the way.

He told her that all he wanted to do was to make her happy.

Anne turned him down as gently as possible.

But Hank wouldn't be deterred. He kept after her, always the well-mannered gentleman, but at the same time, completely determined.

Eventually, he wore her down.

Or more to the point, Anne's circumstances had worn her down. She found out that she was pregnant.

Alarmed and yet thrilled about the baby, she tried to find Dan again. She wasn't any more successful this time around than she had been with her first attempt.

Growing progressively more afraid and feeling completely alone, despite the fact that she did have family back in Rust Creek Falls, she'd accepted Hank's proposal.

But she couldn't marry him until she had told him everything. Summoning all her courage, she'd confessed to Hank that she thought he was a very good man, but that she couldn't love him the way that he loved her. She'd also told him that she was pregnant.

Hank had listened to her very quietly.

When she was finished, he told Anne that none of it made any difference to him. He'd still wanted to marry her. Very much.

Moreover, because it was important to her, he'd wanted her to finish college and get her degree. He'd told her that he was financially comfortable, which meant they could hire someone to look after the baby once he or she was born and she could attend her classes.

They were married shortly after that and Hank was true to his word, hiring a nanny when Janie was born. He wouldn't let anything interfere with Anne finishing college. When she graduated, they came back to Rust Creek Falls. Hank bought a ranch and she found a job as a receptionist at the vet clinic.

For five years, everything seemed to be going well. Hank was good to her and he doted on Janie. He was definitely a good husband and a wonderful father, no one could dispute that, least of all her.

But eventually, Hank came to terms that he was never going to win her over, never get her to love him the way that he had hoped. Because she was in love and would always be in love with Daniel Stockton.

Their divorce was amicable and while

Hank agreed to give her custody of Janie, he reserved the right to see the little girl and to have her over at his ranch whenever he wanted.

His only stipulation for the divorce was that their secret would remain a secret. As far as Janie and everyone else in Rust Creek Falls knew, he was Janie's father. Anne agreed and Hank continued to cherish the role of father.

As for the divorce, though it was sudden, no one really questioned it. Their friends and family all just assumed that she had been too young to get married and that, most important of all, she had married Hank while still on the rebound from Danny.

Anne never told anyone otherwise, thinking it was best for Janie if everyone just went on believing that. That way, they wouldn't go digging any further.

And her secret would remain just that, a secret. There was no reason for it to be otherwise.

Anne sighed as she pushed the memories aside. Instead, she rummaged through her pantry for dinner ingredients, not really sure what it was that she was looking for.

"What's the matter, Mom?" Janie asked.

Anne blinked, realizing that she'd allowed herself to really drift off. She hadn't even heard her daughter come into the kitchen. Facing her now, she quickly offered Janie a smile.

"What makes you ask that? There's nothing the matter, honey," she told her daughter a bit too quickly.

"Yes, there is," Janie insisted. "You've got that funny look on your face, that look you get when something's wrong."

At eleven, Janie looked younger because of her size. She was a shade under four foot ten and weighed seventy-five pounds, making the blue-eyed blonde smaller than average. Despite that, Janie acted older. Sometimes, Anne had the feeling that her daughter was the adult and she was still that young girl who had fallen head over heels for Danny Stockton.

But this was *not* the time to indulge herself or wallow in old memories that belonged locked away in the past.

She knew that Janie was waiting for her to say something. She said the first thing that came to her mind. "I'm just trying to figure out what to make for dinner," she told her daughter. It wasn't exactly the most creative excuse, but for now, it was all she had. "Any suggestions?"

"How about hamburgers?" Janie asked brightly.

Anne shook her head. "Hamburgers are for when I don't really have time to make dinner. The whole point of my coming home early is that I could make you something special."

Far more intuitive than most girls her age, Janie was immediately alert. She looked at her mother suspiciously. "Are you going away, Mom?"

Caught completely off guard, her daughter's question surprised her. Why would Janie think something like that? "No—"

"Am *I* going away?" Janie wanted to know.

Not for the first time, she couldn't help thinking that her daughter was exceptionally bright. Janie could always pick up on her moods and seemed to instinctively know if something was bothering her—sometimes even before *she* knew it.

"No, of course not," Anne denied, making certain that she sounded calm. "Can't a mom come home early and make something special for her best daughter?"

Janie gave her a look as she said, "I'm your only daughter."

"There's that, too," Anne said with a fond laugh as she gave her daughter a one-armed hug. "My best and *only* daughter."

"I like hamburgers, Mom," Janie reminded her pointedly.

Anne surrendered, secretly relieved that she was getting out of this so easily. Janie would normally grill her a lot longer.

"Okay, hamburgers it is," she told her daughter. "But later on, when you're staring down at your plate and you decide that you would have wanted to have something a little fancier, just remember, the hamburgers were your idea."

"I'll remember," Janie promised.

Anne opened the refrigerator to make sure she had the necessary main ingredient for this particular "feast." She did.

"Okay," she said to Janie, closing the refrigerator door again. "Now go do your homework."

"I can do it after dinner," Janie protested, suddenly acting her age again.

"Yes, I know. I also know it's better to get your homework out of the way first so that you don't have it hanging over your head all evening. Remember, your father's coming to pick you up for a sleepover tonight."

Janie sighed dramatically, accepting defeat. "Okay, okay, if you don't want my bright, shining face looking up at you adoringly while you cook, I will go and do my homework."

Eleven, going on thirty, Anne thought with a smile. "Thank you," she said. "I'll see your bright, shining face looking at me from across the dining room table at dinner—*after* you finish your homework."

Janie walked away, shaking her head. "You know, you should have been a teacher, not a receptionist," the little girl complained.

"Oh no," Anne answered, pretending to shudder at the very thought of being a teacher. "Corralling one student is all I can handle. I'd never survive a whole classroom full of them," Anne assured her daughter. "Now go, make me proud."

A giant, deep-down-from-her-toes sigh was her daughter's only response.

Anne's laugh was followed by a soft sigh as another memory corkscrewed through her. Janie was just like Danny had been at that age. Bright, sunny, eager to twist things until he got his way. And he always managed to do it without annoying anyone.

Sometimes, when she looked at Janie, she could really see Danny. See his face, see his mannerisms.

Anne could feel a tightening in the pit of her stomach again.

She supposed that was what had gotten her started today. Remembering what it had been like when she and Danny had been together.

Well, you just stop it right now! she ordered herself fiercely. She didn't have time for this. There was no point in thinking about someone who hadn't been in her life for twelve years.

Anne glanced at her watch. It was still early. Dinner was not for another hour and a half. Since Janie wanted hamburgers, dinner would take no more than fifteen minutes to prepare. That left her with enough time to do something she could actually regard as being fun.

That didn't happen very often.

So infrequently, as a matter of fact, that she couldn't think of anything right off the bat.

Stumped, she was tempted to call her

daughter back into the room. They could watch a program together, one of those cartoons that Janie used to love so much when she was a little girl. Granted Janie was almost an adult—or so her daughter liked to think— but Anne knew that Janie secretly still loved watching animated films, especially the ones that were well made and had heart.

Heaven only knew how much longer that would last, Anne mused, going into the family room and looking at the television guide. It wouldn't be all that long before Janie would feel obligated to turn her back on everything and anything that was connected to the little girl she had once been.

It was a rite of passage, Anne thought sadly.

She was just about to turn on the TV and call her daughter into the family room when she heard the doorbell.

Someone was at her door.

Anne looked at her watch. Ordinarily, she would be still at the animal clinic at this time. Her friends all knew that, which meant that this wasn't a social call. And it was way too early for Hank.

Maybe one of her neighbors had seen that

her car was in the driveway and was bringing over their beloved dog or cat for some free medical advice. For some reason, some of her neighbors thought that just because she worked at the vet clinic, she knew everything that the vets did.

Only one way to find out who was at her door, she thought with a resigned sigh.

She went to the door, preparing to dispatch the neighbor and their pet as quickly as possible.

Opening the door, Anne said, "What seems to be the problem?" before she actually looked at the person who was standing on her doorstep.

The word *problem* came out as more of a squeak than an actual word.

Her heart was suddenly pounding in her ears. Anne blinked, just in case she actually *was* seeing things.

The person on her doorstep didn't vanish, didn't change.

She had imagined this very scene so many times in the last dozen years, she couldn't even begin to count them. Now that it actually seemed to be taking place, she felt as if her entire body had been dipped in glue, then held fast against some invisible canvas. She was unable to move.

Unable to even breathe.

All she could do was stare at him in complete disbelief.

Slowly, she fought back from the emotional paralysis that held her in its grip, struggling to say something, a sentence, a word.

A sound.

"Hello, Anne."

His deep voice rumbled, the sound echoing within her very chest, interfering with the beat of her heart, or what might have passed for a beat right now if it wasn't as paralyzed as the rest of her.

Finally, with the inside of her mouth drier than the desert and swiftly turning into sand, Anne forced herself to say something.

Or rather, to say a word. A name.

His name.

"Danny?" she asked hoarsely, her throat all but closing up.

She saw a smile, that same faint, funny little smile she had loved so well, curve his lips just before he confirmed what she was asking.

"Yes, Anne, it's me."

The moment he said that, she felt them. Felt the tears that she had been harboring within her for the last twelve years, tears she'd forbade herself to ever shed, even once. She had been able to maintain almost superhuman control over herself, afraid that if she ever allowed herself to cry, to shed so much as a single tear, then there would be no way to stop the flow.

Twelve years' worth of tears.

Anne bit her lower lip, desperately trying to prevent them from falling. Struggling to keep from losing the battle she felt she was doomed to lose.

And then she heard him hesitantly say her name again, the name he used to call her, when the world was so full of possibilities and their love was brand-new.

"Annie?"

Chapter 4

In the minutes before he'd knocked on Jamie's door, anticipating the end of a twelve-year separation, Dan had experienced a strong bout of nerves. But he realized now that that had been a piece of cake in comparison to what he'd went through just before he finally rang Annie's doorbell.

For one thing, he hadn't been sure who would be on the other side of that door, Annie or her husband.

Jamie hadn't told him about Annie's marriage when he'd urged him to go see her, but he'd known about Annie's marriage to Hank for a long time now.

He wasn't quite as technologically backward as everyone obviously seemed to think. During one of his bouts of homesickness, he had availed himself of the computer in the ranch town's library and poked around on social media, searching for information about someone he knew.

About Anne.

He himself wasn't on any websites, but that didn't keep him from looking for information about Anne.

And he'd found it.

He found several photos of Annie, her husband and her little girl posted. He remembered the first time he saw the photo of Annie and Hank. It felt as if someone had taken a jagged knife to his chest and savagely carved out his heart. It was also the last time he looked at that site. It hurt too much.

But then he told himself that he had no right to feel that way. He'd left her life; there was no reason to believe she would spend her days pining away for him. He'd left town—and Annie—because he felt he was unworthy of her, felt that he didn't deserve someone as good and pure as her.

That meant that she was free to go on with her life, to marry anyone she chose.

And he was happy for her, happy that she had found someone to love, someone to take care of her. Someone who had obviously started a family with her. He had no right to feel as wounded as he did.

Nonetheless, wounded was how he felt.

And after all these years, there was no denying that he still loved her.

Dan had thought twice about just turning up on her doorstep.

And then he'd thought some more.

However, his need to see Annie again, to just *look* at her outweighed his fear that she would see right through him and guess how he still felt about her.

But that was his problem, not Annie's, and for her sake, he intended to keep his guard up and maintain a tight rein on all those feelings. Above all, he didn't want to risk making her feel uncomfortable in his presence, not for anything in the world.

Annie stared at the man on her doorstep. A thousand questions instantly sprang up in her head, crowding out one another. A thousand questions that she wanted to put to him. But giving voice to any of them would only tear at the scabs that covered wounds which had taken so very long to heal.

And then there was the little girl who was only two rooms away.

Danny's little girl.

It was one thing when she couldn't find Danny to tell him that he was a father, but it was entirely another thing when all that separated Danny from finding out that he was a father was her sudden, very strong onslaught of cold feet.

It went beyond cold feet. Telling him wouldn't just upend Danny's world. Finding out that Danny was Janie's father instead of Hank would cause total chaos in her world, as well.

And then there was Hank to think of.

He'd been good to her. Good when he didn't have to be. She couldn't allow him to be on the receiving end of such a blow. For all intents and purposes, Hank had been Janie's father from the moment the little girl had been born. She hadn't forced the role on Hank; he'd taken it on gladly.

Hank loved their daughter and Janie *was* their daughter. He had raised Janie with her for five years. And then, even after they had gotten a divorce, he hadn't divorced himself from Janie, hadn't taken himself out of her life. He considered himself to be Janie's father even after Anne had told Hank who Janie's real father was. She couldn't just pull the rug out from under him now, not without giving him fair warning.

A *lot* of fair warning.

And yet, here he was, Danny Stockton, like some ghost out of the past, standing on her doorstep. If Janie came into the room, all he would need was to take one look at the little girl and he'd know she was his.

She could feel her stomach tying itself up into a knot.

"What are you doing here?" Anne heard herself finally asking, feeling as if she was trapped in some sort of a surreal dream.

All this time and she hadn't changed a bit, Dan thought, trying not to stare at her. If anything, Annie was even more beautiful than he remembered.

"I was in the neighborhood and thought I'd drop by," Danny answered glibly. "No?"

he asked, seeing the look on her face. He shrugged, feeling awkward, something he'd never felt around her before. "Well, it was worth a shot. The truth is, I saw a clip on TV a month ago. Jamie and his triplets were in it. After the program was over, I couldn't stop seeing their faces. I knew I had to come back to Rust Creek Falls to see them."

You had to come back to see them. But not me. "Oh, I see," Anne murmured, her voice stilted.

"And you," Dan added awkwardly, realizing his oversight. "I wanted to see you." He blew out a ragged breath and then asked, "Can I come in?"

For a moment, it looked as if she was going to say no. But then she stepped back and gestured for him to enter the house.

"Mom?" Janie called out. She ventured into the living room and looked uncertainly at the stranger talking to her mother.

For the second time in as many minutes, Anne felt her heart lodge itself in her throat as she all but stopped breathing.

Could Danny see it? Could he see that Janie was his daughter?

She slanted a hesitant look in his direction. Danny was smiling broadly at the little girl.

"Hi. You must be Janie," he said. There was clearly awe in his eyes.

The picture of confidence and self-assurance, Janie raised her chin. "I am. Who are you?" she wanted to know.

"Janie," Anne chided her daughter for responding so bluntly.

"No, that's okay," Danny was quick to tell her. "She's being direct. That's a very positive quality to have." He turned his attention to the little girl. "I'm Daniel Stockton," he told her. "I used to live in Rust Creek Falls."

"And you were friends with my mom?" Janie asked, curious.

Anne felt a sharp pang in her heart, afraid of saying anything. Afraid of giving herself away.

He looked at Anne for a moment before he answered. "Yes," he replied quietly. "I was friends with your mom."

"And my dad?" Janie wanted to know, probing further.

"No," Dan answered truthfully. "I'm afraid that I never met your dad."

Growing progressively more apprehensive,

Anne didn't want this exchange to go any further. Not until she set a few ground rules to make sure that nothing was exposed ahead of time.

Until then, she needed to keep Janie and Danny away from one another.

"Did you finish your homework, young lady?" she asked her daughter.

"No, not yet," Janie began. "But—"

Anne cut her off. "Then I suggest you go back and finish it. That's what we agreed to, remember?" she reminded her daughter.

Janie made a face. "I don't remember agreeing," she protested. "You just told me to do it."

"Same thing, puddin'," Anne told her daughter affectionately. "Now go," she said, pointing toward the rear of the house where Janie's room was located, "and don't come back until you've finished doing it."

"Yes, ma'am," Janie sighed with a pout. Turning, she dragged her feet as she went to her room.

"She looks like you."

So worried that he'd see himself in their daughter, Anne didn't hear him at first. And then his words replayed themselves in her head. She turned around to face Danny, a little stunned.

"What?"

"I said she looks like you." There was no missing the fondness in his voice. Or the wistfulness. "A miniature carbon copy of what you looked like at that age. She's what, about nine, right?"

Nine would make her safe, Anne thought. If Danny thought that Janie was nine, then he'd definitely believe that the little girl was Hank's daughter and that would be that. Fear of discovery would be taken off the table once and for all.

But saying yes would be lying, Anne thought and somehow, she just couldn't bring herself to lie to Danny after all these years.

The word stuck in her throat like a fishbone that had been accidentally swallowed.

Rather than say yes or no, Anne focused on something else he had just said. "You really think she looks like me?"

"Absolutely," he assured her. "Right down to her stubborn streak."

"What does a stubborn streak look like?" Anne asked wryly.

Dan smiled at her, fighting a very strong

desire to touch her. Not in the intimate way he used to—after all, she was another man's wife now—but just to put his hand on her shoulder, to connect with her for the smallest of moments.

"I'm looking at it right now," he told Annie. And then his smile faded as he grew serious. "When you opened the door just now, you asked me what I was doing here."

Anne inclined her head, slightly embarrassed. "Not exactly the politest way to greet someone after twelve years," she admitted, then went on to say, "but in my defense, you did catch me by surprise."

Lord, but she looked good, he couldn't help thinking, all but devouring her with his eyes. "You know, I didn't exactly tell you the truth when I said I was in the neighborhood."

"I had my suspicions," she replied with a soft laugh. Rust Creek Falls was in no one's neighborhood. "So why are you here?" she asked.

Dan cleared his voice before saying, "I came to apologize for leaving you the way I did."

Stunned by his admission, Anne looked at the man she had once thought of as the love of her life. It took her more than a moment to find her tongue.

"You know, over the last dozen years, I must have imagined this scene a hundred different ways. The only thing all those scenes had in common, besides your apology, was that I always felt relieved when I heard you apologize. I felt somehow vindicated.

"But I'm not vindicated, not relieved," she told him with feeling. "I'm just…sad, I guess. Sad about all the years in between that were lost. Why did you leave like that?"

Dan shook his head. That was something he didn't want to get into. It was a secret he would most likely take to his grave rather than burden someone else with.

"I didn't have a choice," was all he allowed himself to say.

Anne frowned ever so slightly. That excuse just didn't hold any water for her. "Everyone always has a choice," she told him.

"*I* didn't," he replied.

There had to be more, something he wasn't telling her. "But—"

Dan changed the subject. "I also wanted to tell you that I'm happy for you."

For a moment, still trying to understand

what Danny wasn't telling her, she was caught off guard. His last words completely confused her.

"What did you say?"

"I said I'm happy for you," Danny repeated. "Happy that you've moved on. That you found someone you cared about and got married. That you went on to have a beautiful daughter."

She's your beautiful daughter, she thought, an unexpected wave of anger filling her.

Anne continued staring at him. "You're happy for me," she repeated in disbelief, like someone who didn't quite understand the gist of the words she was saying.

Dan nodded, forcing a smile to his lips. "Yes, I am."

Did he even have a clue how much it stung to hear him say that to her? How much it actually physically tore her apart?

Why didn't you come back to me? Why didn't you show up on my doorstep years ago and tell me that you couldn't bear to live without me? Why did you just vanish out of my life without a trace, leaving me to face being pregnant all by myself?

But she couldn't say any of that, couldn't

risk him knowing the truth, at least not yet. Perhaps not ever. There were other people to consider.

So, instead, she asked, "Where were you all these years?"

Anne struggled to keep the accusation out of her voice, doing her best to sound like just an old friend trying to catch up with another old friend instead of a spurned lover who'd given her heart away and had it torn in two more than a decade ago.

Dan looked at her, wondering how to reply to her question. There wasn't that much to tell her, really. For all intents and purposes, his life had ended the day he had left town with his brothers.

"Wyoming first," he finally said. "Then Colorado."

She could almost picture him going to Wyoming if she tried. But not Colorado.

"Colorado?" Anne echoed. "What did you do there?" she asked.

"Actually, I'm still there," he told her. "I took a temporary leave of absence to come out here," he said, then went on to answer her question. "I'm a sales manager for an exclusive dude ranch."

"A dude ranch?" It seemed like such an unlikely place for him to land, Anne thought. "What does a sales manager do at a dude ranch?"

He laughed dryly. "Mainly I put together vacation packages for burned-out city slickers who think that riding around on a horse for a couple of weeks, pretending to be Roy Rogers, is guaranteed to make a whole new man out of them."

The mocking tone of his voice had her wondering other things. "Are you happy?" she wanted to know.

He shrugged and smiled. "It's a living."

"That's not what I asked," she told him, wondering if he was purposely trying to be evasive. Was he unhappy? Had he been as unhappy as she had?

"The pay's good and the dude ranch reminds me of the Sunshine Farm," he told her, referring to the ranch where he and his siblings had lived while growing up—before his parents were killed.

"Are you going back?" she asked him. "To the dude ranch," she specified when she realized that she hadn't been clear.

He hadn't worked that out in his head yet.

He still had his job waiting for him and part of him had every intention of returning to Colorado. But seeing Jamie and his family—seeing her—had caused all sorts of doubts to spring up in his head.

"Well, I—" he began hesitantly, not wanting to lie, but not wanting to mislead her, either.

Just then, the doorbell rang, curtailing any further conversation between them.

Anne wanted to ignore it, wanted him to finish answering her question as to whether or not he would be leaving her again. Suddenly, she felt on the verge of telling Danny about Janie even though she knew it would be like dropping a bombshell on him.

But it also might be just the incentive he needed to convince him to stay in Rust Creek Falls.

The doorbell rang again.

Dan looked at her quizzically. "Aren't you going to answer that?" he asked her.

When the doorbell rang a third time, she fixed a smile on her face, said, "Sure," and then went to answer the door.

Before she reached it, she heard the sound of her daughter running into the room. For such a slight little girl, she had very heavy feet and the ability to make her presence known, Anne thought.

"In case that's Dad, I've got my bag all packed and ready," Janie announced cheerfully.

"That's good, dear. You wouldn't want to keep your father waiting," Anne told her daughter as she opened the door.

Hank Harlow walked in.

Chapter 5

The first person Hank Harlow saw when Anne opened the door to admit him in was not his ex-wife, nor was it the little girl who'd had him completely wrapped around her little finger from the moment she was born. It was the tall, lanky cowboy in the room. The one standing near Anne.

The man who had been his competition, sight unseen, all these years.

His dark eyes darted back to Anne, an unspoken question in his pointed look.

Anne knew what her ex-husband was silently asking her and very slowly, she shook her head just enough to let him know that she hadn't said anything to either Dan or to the little girl Hank considered his daughter.

The next second Janie had launched herself into Hank's arms, eager for their evening together to get started.

"Hi, Dad!"

"Hi yourself, Short Stuff," Hank responded affectionately, hugging the little girl who had her arms tightly wrapped around his waist.

These were the moments to savor, Hank thought. Even if he wasn't looking at a very real threat to his fragile world right here in his ex-wife's living room, it wouldn't be all that long before Janie became a teenager. Teenagers weren't all that keen on public displays of affection when it came to their dads.

He was going to miss this.

"I packed early," Janie told him proudly as she finally dropped her hands to her sides.

Hank saw the stuffed backpack she'd dropped on the floor as she'd run to hug him. "That's my girl," he said with approval, ruffling her hair.

His words carried a slight territorial ring to them, Dan noted. Obviously, the man thought he was here to try to break up his family, but he would never do anything like that. He'd had his chance twelve years ago and he'd missed it, Dan thought.

Stepping forward, he put his hand out to the man who had his arm still protective around Janie's shoulders. "Hi, I'm Dan Stockton," he said, introducing himself.

"Yes, I know," Hank replied frostily. After a beat, he took Dan's hand and barely shook it before let it drop. "I'm Hank Harlow." He slanted a quick, meaningful glance in Anne's direction as he added, "Janie's dad."

"C'mon, Dad, let's go," Janie urged, tugging on Hank's hand as she turned in the direction of the front door.

"Don't forget to take your schoolbooks with you," Anne reminded her daughter.

Janie pointed toward the bulging backpack. "They're in there, Mom," she assured her mother. "I just packed them."

"Homework, too?" Anne stressed.

Janie signed dramatically as if it irritated her to be treated like a child. "Homework, too."

Anne smiled at her. "Then I guess you're all set," she concluded. "We'll have those hamburgers another night."

"I'll bring her to school in the morning," Hank made a point of telling her.

Anne nodded. Crossing to the duo at the door, she kissed the top of her daughter's head. "Behave yourself," she said affectionately.

"She always behaves herself," Hank said. "Short Stuff's perfect."

Janie beamed as she looked up at him. She tugged on his hand again, more urgently this time.

"Let's go!" she pleaded insistently.

"Have a good time," Anne called after her daughter.

Janie waved at her as she ran to the car.

She watched as Hank opened the passenger door for Janie. Once the girl was strapped in, he shut the door and rounded the hood to the driver's side. He paused to give her one last warning look before getting into his truck himself.

Anne could tell from her ex-husband's expression that he clearly didn't want her saying anything to Dan about Janie being his daughter. She knew how Hank felt about Janie, knew he feared that if the truth came out, he might lose Janie's love.

She sincerely doubted that would happen, but she could understand his concern.

Watching Hank, she bit her lower lip, utterly torn between the truth and her sense of loyalty.

She continued watching until Hank started up the truck and then pulled away from her house.

With a sigh, she closed the front door and then turned around to face Dan. Her heart hammering, she was acutely aware of the fact that they were now completely alone in the house.

For a moment, she wasn't sure just what to say to him, how to even begin a conversation.

The question Dan asked her the next moment didn't help, either. "When did you get divorced?"

Her mouth felt like dry cotton. How did he know? *How could he not know? Hank was picking Janie up for an overnight stay. Only divorced parents do that sort of thing, idiot*, she upbraided herself.

"You didn't know?" Anne asked, doing her best to sound nonchalant.

"I didn't even know you were married until I started prowling through social media, looking to see if I could find any photos or information on you. I came across pictures of you and Janie—and him," Dan told her, remembering how much it had hurt, seeing her with Hank, so much so that he never went back. But he wasn't about to tell her that. "But, funny thing, there aren't pictures posted that can capture a divorce."

She didn't want to have this conversation, afraid that she might accidentally let something slip before she was ready—assuming she would ever be ready.

Taking a breath, she deliberately ignored his question regarding her divorce and switched gears to act like a hostess.

"Can I offer you something to drink? Coffee, a soft drink, water?" she asked, doing her best to keep her voice light.

Dan understood what she was telling him. That this topic was off-limits. He could respect that. Divorces could wound a person far more effectively than a bullet. He had his untouchable subjects and she had hers, he thought, so he backed off.

"No, I'm fine," Dan assured her.

"Something to eat, then?" she offered. "I've got some leftover fried chicken in the refrigerator—I made it," she told him, then made a point of adding, "I've learned to cook better now."

"There was nothing wrong with the way you cooked," Dan said kindly.

She laughed a little, some of the tension between them temporarily backing off. "That was because you were in love with me back then."

I'm still in love with you, he silently told her. Out loud, Dan contradicted her. "Bad cooking has a way of cutting through that," he assured her. Knowing a little shot of honesty was called for here, he added, "You weren't going to make Martha Stewart pack up her pots and pans, but you weren't bad."

"So then, can I get you something to eat? I could make hamburgers," she offered, already crossing to the refrigerator, eager to do something with her hands. Preparing a light dinner would take care of that.

His stomach felt so tied up in knots, Dan knew if he consumed something, he ran the serious risk of having it come back up.

Maybe it was time to leave, he told himself.

"No, really, I'm fine. I didn't come here to eat," he told Anne. "I really did just come to apologize. And now that I have, I should get going." Needing a way to gracefully pave his way out, he grabbed at the first thing that occurred to him. "I promised Jamie I'd be back by a certain time. If I'm not there when I said I would be, I don't want him thinking I've taken off for another twelve years."

"That's very thoughtful of you," Anne told him stiffly.

About to leave, he took Anne's hand for a moment, only to have her pull it back as if she'd just been touched by a hot poker. And then he saw her flush, her cheeks turning a shade of pink he would have found infinitely appealing if it wasn't for the fact that she had just acted as if she couldn't stand being touched by him.

This was going to take time and patience, he told himself—if he wound up staying, he added, and that hadn't been decided yet.

"I really am sorry, Annie," he told her quietly. And then he crossed to the door and opened it.

"Wait!"

Dan slowly turned around, waiting, a silent query in his eyes.

"You can't— I mean, when—" She

sounded tongue-tied, till she finally said, "Will I see you again?"

"If I decide to go back to Colorado, I'll stop by to let you know and say goodbye," he promised.

And with that, he turned away from her and left.

He heard Anne flip the lock on the door. It had a prophetic, final sound to it.

Trying to shake off the thought, he hurried to his truck.

"So, how did it go?"

Jamie's question met him the moment Dan walked through the door his brother held open.

"Have you been standing there this entire time?" Dan wanted to know, walking across the threshold.

"Not standing," Jamie corrected, and then he admitted, "Pacing, maybe."

"This whole time?" Dan asked again. Was his brother that uncertain that he would return?

"No," Jamie answered defensively—and then he relented. "Just for the last hour. So how did it go?" he repeated.

Dan walked into the living room. He expected to find his newfound nephews and niece in the room, or, at the very least, his new sister-in-law.

But the room was empty.

Dan sank down on the sofa and looked at his brother, waiting for him to sit down beside him. He'd heard the nervousness in Jamie's voice. It didn't take a rocket scientist to guess the reason behind it. Did Jamie expect him to be angry?

It was best to get this out of the way sooner than later, he thought. "You didn't tell me Annie had gotten married."

He saw the apprehension in Jamie's eyes as his brother answered, "I was afraid you wouldn't go see her if you knew about that."

And it was obviously important to Jamie that he saw Anne, Dan thought, still somewhat mystified. "Why did you want me to go see her?"

"Because you wanted to," Jamie answered simply. And then he added with emphasis, "And I think that you needed to."

"Is that why you didn't tell me about the little girl, too?" Dan guessed, doing his best to try to piece everything together.

Jamie blew out a breath. "Yes," he admitted. "I'm sorry I kept that from you, but—"

Dan raised his hand, not letting him finish. "And the divorce?" he asked, focusing on the final point. "Why didn't you tell me that she was divorced?"

"Because if I told you that, I would have had to tell you that she'd gotten married first and I didn't want to get into any of that. Besides, I wanted Anne to tell you about her divorce herself." An almost sheepish smile curved the corners of his mouth. "I figured you'd get the good news after you weathered the bad. Bottom line is that Annie's a free woman. The rest of it is just history."

"History that produced a little girl," Dan pointed out.

Jamie didn't know how his brother felt about that part, but he was not about to get into an argument with Dan. Not after Dan had only just now come back into his life after more than a decade's hiatus.

He deliberately focused on the positive aspect.

"Janie's a real cutie, isn't she?" Jamie asked.

For a long moment, Dan remained silent.

And then he slowly smiled and said, "She's Annie's daughter. How could she not be?"

"I know, right?" Jamie asked. Getting up, he crossed over to the small liquor cabinet in the corner. He poured two shots of Wild Turkey and brought them both over to the sofa, placing one on the coffee table in front of Dan. "What did Annie say when she opened the door and saw you standing there?"

"Her exact words were 'What are you doing here?'" he told Jamie.

Jamie laughed, shaking his head. "That's Annie, direct as ever." He nodded at the untouched shot glass. "Would you like something else instead?" he asked. "My liquor cabinet's not well stocked, but I've got a few different things you can chose from," Jamie told him, getting up again.

But Dan shook his head. "That's okay, don't trouble yourself. I don't drink."

Jamie looked at him in surprise. He'd never actually seen Dan drink. However, one of the last nights they were still a real family, he remembered that Dan, Luke and Bailey had snuck out to a bar to go drinking.

"You don't drink?" he repeated. "Seriously?" he asked his brother.

"Seriously," Dan replied.

"Not ever?"

"No," Dan answered stoically.

Jamie put down the shot glass he was just about to raise to his own lips. He wasn't going to have a drink if Dan wasn't.

"Since when?" he asked.

Dan wasn't all that eager to talk about it, but then, he knew he couldn't keep running from this forever. Because he had things to hide, he fed Jamie the barest information.

"Since the night Mom and Dad died," Dan told him simply.

"Because they were killed by that drunk driver," Jamie guessed.

That wasn't the reason, but Dan let it go at that. Because if he didn't, if he told Jamie that wasn't the real reason, he would have to explain further and let Jamie in on the terrible secret he'd been carrying around with him for the last twelve years.

It was enough that he was burdened with that secret. He wasn't about to tell Jamie and have him share the burden. Jamie didn't deserve to have to put up with that.

So instead, he nodded his head and said, "Yeah, something like that. But you don't have to abstain just because I'm not drinking," he told Jamie, nodding at the drink that his brother had set down.

"They were my parents, too," Jamie needlessly reminded him.

Yeah, and I'm the reason they're not here right now. I'm the reason you and Bella had to put up with being raised—if you can call it that—by Grandma and Grandpa while the other girls were adopted and farmed out. I'm the reason Luke and Bailey had to leave home and why our whole family wound up being shattered and split up.

Though he had kept his silence all these years, it still felt as if the secret was cutting him up with small, jagged knives.

"Hey, what's the matter?" Jamie asked. "You look like you've just seen a ghost." Compassion filled him as he put his hand on his brother's shoulder. "Danny, talk to me. Are you okay?"

"Just a little emotionally wrung out, I guess," Danny told him. "I just need some rest. I'll be fine by morning," he promised.

Jamie looked at the clock on the mantel. "It's a little early for bed," he noted. "Don't you want to have some dinner first? Fallon's putting together this Prodigal Brother Returns Feast, guaranteed to knock your socks off. Are you sure you want to miss that?" Jamie asked him.

Dan really wanted some time to himself to process everything that had happened today. But at the same time, he didn't want to insult his new sister-in-law or hurt her feelings by taking a pass on dinner. Especially after she had gone to all this trouble for him. That wouldn't be right.

"No, I surely don't want to miss that," he told Jamie. "It's not every day that I have a feast in my honor."

"So you'll have dinner with us?" Jamie asked, looking at him hopefully.

"Hey, I wouldn't miss it for the world," Dan assured him.

The expression that came over Jamie's face was the epitome of happiness as well as relief.

Chapter 6

Dan couldn't remember the last meal he'd had with family, and he didn't want this one to end. But it was getting late and he was exhausted.

Pushing aside his now cold coffee, he was about to call it a night when his brother finally brought up the subject that had been on Dan's mind all throughout the meal.

"You know," Jamie said, leaning in to him, "when Hank divorced Anne, she came to see me, as well as Bella, asking if either one of us had finally heard from you and knew where you were." He sighed, shaking his head. "Of course, we couldn't help her because we had no idea where you—"

"Wait," Dan cried incredulously, interrupting his brother. "Hank divorced her?"

"Yes." Jamie looked at him quizzically. "You said that you knew they had gotten divorced. Why do you look so surprised?"

"Well, yes, I knew they were divorced, but I thought that Annie was the one who had divorced Hank," Dan answered.

He frowned, confused as he tried to figure the situation out. How could Hank, after getting someone like Anne to marry him, throw all that away and actually divorce her? That just didn't make any sense to him. In Hank's place, no reason in the world would have made him do that.

He put the question to Jamie. "Why would Hank divorce her?"

"Well, I don't know any of the particulars," Jamie confessed, "but if I had to make a guess, off the top of my head I'd say that Hank finally came to terms with the fact that Annie was still in love with you and always would be. He didn't want to continue in second place."

Dan thought back to the awkwardness of

his first meeting with Anne after all this time, and the way she had pulled back when he'd tried to take her hand. He made a small, dismissive guttural sound.

"I think you might have been kicked in the head by one of those horses you like to baby."

Jamie shrugged. "Make jokes all you want, but I have a very strong feeling that I'm right about this," he told Dan.

"I wouldn't try to argue him out of that if I were you," Fallon advised as she rose to clear away the dishes from the table. "Jamie might look mild-mannered, but once he gets something into his head, there's no budging him."

"All right, then I won't try," Dan told his sister-in-law agreeably. "Even though he *is* dead wrong. Here, let me help you with that," he offered, reaching for the plates Fallon had just stacked.

"Don't you dare," she warned Dan, a smile belying the sharp tone she'd taken. She swatted Dan's hand away from the dishes. "In case you've forgotten, you're a guest here."

"I'm crashing at your place and taking full advantage of your kindness. That means I owe you—big time—and should do something to earn my keep," Dan pointed out.

Fallon sighed, surrendering the plates to him. "Looks like Jamie isn't the only stubborn Stockton here." Her smile grew wider as Dan cleared the table. "I think I could get used to this."

Just then, one of the triplets decided to make themselves known. "Uh-oh. Sounds like duty calls," she told the two brothers, glancing toward the source of the cries. "I'd better see what's going on before all three of them wake up."

"It was a wonderful dinner, Fallon," Dan called after her. "Thank you."

"Jamie, make sure you tell your brother he can stay with us as long as he likes," Fallon tossed over her shoulder as she walked upstairs to check on which of the triplets wanted to be fed or changed.

"You know, Jamie, you've got it made," Dan told his brother enviously as the latter followed him, carrying another large batch of plates and utensils to the kitchen sink.

"I do, but I didn't always," Jamie responded. "I thought my life was over when Paula died, leaving me with three infants to raise. I felt like the bottom had completely dropped out of my world," he confided.

He looked at Dan, deliberately making his point. "But I hung on, determined to be there for my kids, to make them as happy as I possibly could. I wasn't prepared to find love again, but somehow, it found *me*." He gave his brother an encouraging smile. "And you'll get there, too, Danny. Just hang in there and don't give up."

Danny shrugged the advice away. "I missed my chance and I know it," he replied, totally convinced of what he was saying.

Danny might have been convinced, but Jamie didn't see it that way.

"You're still breathing, aren't you?" Jamie asked, rinsing off the plates before stacking them on the counter on the way to the dishwasher.

"Yeah, but—" Danny began to protest.

Jamie talked right over him, not wanting to hear any excuses. "And so's Annie."

Danny sighed. "It's not that simple, Jamie," he insisted.

"It's not that complicated, either, Danny. Like they say, where there's life, there's hope."

For a moment Danny was silent, then he brightened as he turned to Jamie.

"Tell you what, brother," he said. "Instead

of putting these dishes into the dishwasher, why don't we just handle this the old-fashioned way? You wash and I'll dry. This way, you can surprise Fallon when she comes back out into the kitchen to start the dishwasher."

Jamie knew what Danny was trying to do, but he'd said what he'd wanted to say and for now he let the subject drop. The Danny he had grown up with had been quick to smile and quick to lend a helping hand, but reaching out to his onetime love was something Danny would have to mull over before he finally decided to make a move.

All Jamie could do was plant the seed in Danny's head and fervently hope that with enough time, it would germinate.

"Fallon'd like that," Jamie said, agreeing to the suggestion.

"Well then, let's get to it," Danny responded, turning up the water.

Jamie's comment to him about the situation with Annie not being as complicated as he felt it was kept replaying itself in his head until he finally fell asleep that night. And they were the first words that sprang into his head the following morning.

Thoughts of Annie were temporarily put

on hold, though when shortly after breakfast Dan heard the front door burst open, someone demanding, "Where is he?" and before he knew what was happening, he found himself enveloped in a huge embrace from behind.

"You're here. You're really here!" an excited female voice exclaimed. When he managed to shift in his seat—and the embrace—he discovered that he was being hugged by his sister Bella.

Sitting opposite him, Jamie grinned. "Told you she'd be happy to see you."

"Talk to me," Bella cried, making herself comfortable in the chair next to his. "Tell me everything!"

Which was how Dan wound up spending the rest of the day, talking to his sister and catching up on her life. A life which he was happy to learn had ultimately fared better than his had.

Dana, taking a quick trip from Portland, came to see him the day after that, and although there was less squealing, it almost an instant replay of the day before.

Both days were filled with the stuff that emotional, happy reunions were made of.

But all those stirred-up emotions caused

thoughts of Annie to creep back into his brain, haunting him during the late evening even though he tried his best to ignore them.

Dan sought refuge in work. He volunteered and worked beside Jamie on the range, doing his best to forget about Annie.

At breakfast the fourth day Jamie leaned over the table toward him and said, "You know, I've got an awful lot to take care of on the ranch today—"

The admission was like music to Dan's ears. Keeping busy was the best way he knew of to keep from thinking and torturing himself with would-be scenarios that all began with "what if."

"Just tell me what you need done and I'll do it," Dan was quick to offer.

Jamie got up from the table and went to the writing desk that was nestled in the alcove between the kitchen and the small dining room.

"This will be a real time-saver for me," Jamie told him.

Dan was still seated at the table, finishing the last of his second cup of extra-dark coffee. He heard a drawer being opened and then closed again. Half a beat later, Jamie walked back into the kitchen holding an envelope in his hand. The name of the veterinary clinic in town was written across the front: Dr. Brooks Smith's Veterinary Clinic.

"I need to make a payment on my vet bill," he told Dan, holding out the envelope. "Would you mind very much bringing it into town for me?"

"Wouldn't I be more useful helping you out here, on the ranch?" Dan questioned.

"Trust me, this'll take a big load off my mind. You know how I feel about owing someone," he reminded his brother.

A smile played on his lips as fragments of distant childhood memories returned. "Vaguely," Danny said, tongue in cheek.

"Well, I've only gotten worse." He pressed the envelope into Danny's hand. "Do you mind?"

It really seemed important to him, Dan thought, so he took the envelope and slipped it into his shirt pocket.

"Of course not. Consider it done." Habit had him checking his pocket for the keys to his Jeep as he rose from the table. "I'll be back as soon as I can," he promised.

"Take your time," Jamie told him. "The work's not going anywhere."

Dan took his jacket off the hook by the

front door. Putting it on, he gave his brother a quick wave and left the house.

"You're terrible," Fallon told her husband the moment Dan closed the door.

Jamie gave his wife a wide-eyed look. "What makes you say that?"

Fallon rolled her eyes. "Don't play innocent with me. You could have just as easily put that check in the mail."

Jamie pretended to find the suggestion lacking. "I've always found the personal touch to be the better way to go," he told his wife.

"Ha! You just want Danny to walk into the vet clinic so that he can see Annie when he hands your check to her."

"Well, that's definitely the personal touch, isn't it?" he asked her, daring his wife to possibly suggest otherwise.

"There's no arguing with that," Fallon agreed. "But I'm not sure if Danny's going to appreciate being manipulated."

"He will," Jamie said confidently. "Once he comes to his senses," he added. He looked at Fallon, wanting his wife to side with him. "Someone's got to make the first move."

"Don't you think it should be one of the two people involved in this?" Fallon asked.

"It should," Jamie readily agreed. "But when that doesn't look like it's about to happen, sometimes a little divine intervention is necessary."

"Divine intervention?" Fallon repeated, laughter in her eyes. "Meaning you?"

"Hey, if the description fits..." His voice trailed off as a whimsical expression played hide-and-seek on his face.

Fallon shook her head. But he knew there was no way she could be exasperated with him. Not when he was obviously attempting to do a good thing for his brother.

"I love you, Jamie Stockton," she said.

His eyes softened as he looked at her. "I know," he told her. "And I love you, too."

Just then, not one, not two but all three very loud, plaintive voices blended, creating an indignant, highly unhappy chorus.

"Sounds like our children are calling," Fallon said as she got up from the table.

"Calling?" he echoed. "I'd say that it sounds more like they're bellowing," Jamie told her. "C'mon," he urged his wife. "I'll help. There's supposed to be safety in numbers."

"Safety?" she laughed. "Not hardly. In case you hadn't noticed, it's two to three. That means that those little critters still outnumber us."

"We can brazen it out," he told her as if they were actually planning strategy to use against their babies. "Remember, when we enter the room, don't make any eye contact. They can detect fear a mile away. It'll only go downhill from there if they do."

Fallon shook her head. "You should write a book on raising triplets," she teased.

"Maybe I will," Jamie responded, pretending to mull the idea over. "All I need to do is to learn how to type."

"That would mean that you would have to change and I don't want you to change even a single thing about yourself," Fallon told him with a great deal of affection in her tone. "I love you just the way you are."

"Good to know," Jamie said as he kissed her. It was all the fortification he needed to deal with their brood.

Rust Creek Falls had done some growing since he had left it, Dan thought as he drove into the heart of town. The place had more stores than when he'd lived there, but the ones that he did recognize reminded him of the same sleepy little town that it had been.

The town vet had been part of that expansion, going from what had been essentially a one-man show to a clinic. The word *clinic* suggested at least more than one vet, Dan mused. And that was a good thing, as he suspected that the ranches in the area had done their own growing. More cattle and horses meant that more of them needed looking after.

There was a time when a rancher would do his best for his livestock and then just allow nature to take over, tipping the scales one way or another. Now ranchers relied on vets to keep the scales tipped in their favor, but there were fees for that, he mused, thinking of the envelope he had tucked into his pocket.

He was surprised that Jamie had asked him to run the payment into town for him rather than just putting it in the mail, but then he gathered that mail service hadn't kept up with growth quite the way other things had. Besides, he didn't mind being useful. It was one thing to be earning a paycheck, and another thing to feel useful to someone who counted.

He preferred the latter.

Dan scanned both sides of the street as he

slowly made his way through the town, taking note of a couple of new restaurants that had opened up. There was a new bar, too, but that held no interest for him, nudging at memories he didn't want stirred. He kept his eyes peeled for the vet clinic.

He finally spotted it after traveling more than halfway through Rust Creek Falls. In one of the older buildings in town, the clinic didn't create much of an impression at first sight, but then, it didn't have to, he thought. All it had to do was keep good veterinarians in its employ.

There was parking for the clinic across the way and he chose a spot closest to the building. Getting out of the Jeep, he didn't bother locking it. If anyone was going to steal a vehicle, Dan figured that they wouldn't bother with one that had as many miles on it as his did.

He made his way to the clinic's front door and went right in. The receptionist's desk was front and center, visible the second he stepped inside the building.

There was no one ahead of him so he stepped right up to the desk. The greeting he was about to offer died on his lips as the receptionist turned her chair around to face him.

Annie.

Chapter 7

Annie was speechless.

It took her more than a moment to collect herself. Her accelerating pulse, however, was a whole other story. But at least Danny had no way of knowing that it was currently going faster than a NASCAR racer, she thought, and all because of him.

When she finally regained the ability to form words, she bluntly asked him, "How did you know I work here?" She was grateful that at least her voice hadn't cracked at the last second.

"I didn't," Dan answered.

But obviously Jamie did, he realized. Now his brother's unusual request to run into town and make a payment in person made sense.

His younger brother had a lot of explaining to do once Dan got back to the ranch.

Anne assessed his response. Taking a breath, she peered at him over the desk. "If you didn't know I'd be here, then what are you doing here?" As far as she could tell, he didn't have an animal in tow.

"Jamie sent me," Dan answered. Then, almost as an afterthought, he added, "He asked me to drop off his monthly installment on his vet bill."

"Monthly installment?" she repeated, looking at him in confusion.

"That's what he said," Danny told her, handing over the envelope that his brother asked him to deliver.

Annie set the envelope down next to her computer. He watched as her finely shaped eyebrows drew together in perplexed consternation while her fingers flew across the keyboard.

"Something wrong?" he asked Annie, already sensing that something had to be off.

Unwilling to get specific just yet, she merely told Dan, "Just checking."

But she'd aroused his curiosity. There had to be a reason for that doubtful expression on her face. "Checking what?"

She didn't bother looking up. Instead, she evasively said, "If I made a mistake."

"A mistake," he echoed, waiting for some more information. When Annie said nothing further, his curiosity doubled in proportion. "In the accounting in general," Dan pressed, "or—?"

Annie slanted a glance at him. This felt awkward all around. Why couldn't he just back off like a normal person?

Because he wasn't a "normal" person, she reminded herself. He was Danny and everything that entailed. He didn't just go along with things; he had to have them spelled out.

"I'm afraid I'm going to have to go with 'or,'" she told him.

He laughed dryly as he watched her type on the keyboard.

"I guess a lot of things have changed in the last twelve years," he remarked. "When did you learn to talk in code like that?"

The phone rang at that moment, preventing

her from answering him. One eye still on the computer screen, she picked up the receiver.

"Brooks Smith's Veterinary Clinic," she answered as she put her finger up, indicating to Dan that their conversation was temporarily on hold. "How may I help you?"

For the next minute or so Annie questioned and advised the person on the other end of the call.

She sounded so self-assured, Dan thought. When he'd left Rust Creek Falls with his brothers, he'd left behind a sweet, loving, shy teenage girl who'd just touched the edges of self-discovery. He was looking at a woman now, a woman who had obviously known love, and pain, and during all that, managed to raise a daughter who reflected well on her.

"If you're willing to wait until four," Annie was saying to whoever was on the other end of the call, "I can have Brooks come out to your place to take a look at your mare." She listened to the person's response. "Good, I'll let the doctor know. He'll be at the ranch around four o'clock."

Hanging up, she turned her attention back to him.

"Now can you tell me what you were talking about?" he asked Annie.

Her eyes darted back to the computer screen. "Well, it's just that—"

The door behind him opened and they were interrupted again. Dan heard someone coming in. From the sound of it, the person wasn't alone. Danny didn't have to turn around to know that. He'd suddenly found himself to be a person of interest for an overly energetic bloodhound who all but inhaled him.

"Heel, Bowser," a gruff voice behind him ordered. The bloodhound behaved as if no command had been issued, sniffing that much harder and all but climbing up on the side of Dan's leg. "I said heel, damn it!" the man behind Dan said, irritated. "I'm sorry about this," he apologized when Dan turned around.

"Mr. Mayfield," Anne addressed the bloodhound's owner as she got up from behind her desk and came around to the front. "Why don't we check Bowser's weight and then you can take him into the second room to wait for the doctor?" she suggested, making her way to an oversize scale in the corner just beyond the front door.

But the bloodhound hadn't quite gotten

over his fascination with Danny. "Why don't I walk over to the scale?" he suggested to the dog's owner. "It might make things easier for everyone."

"I'm sorry," Mr. Mayfield apologized. "Bowser's usually better behaved than this."

The man gladly took Dan up on his suggestion, holding tightly onto the bloodhound's leash as Bowser followed Dan right to the scale.

Confronted with the scale, the bloodhound only put three of his four paws down on the scale. It took three tries and all three of them to get all four of the dog's paws onto the scale at the same time in order to get an accurate reading.

Closest to the readout, Dan looked down at the numbers and announced, "One hundred and twenty-nine pounds."

"You can take Bowser to room two," Anne declared. Mr. Mayfield set off down the hall and she returned to her chair behind the desk. She looked a little frazzled and her hair was falling into her eyes.

Seeing her like that conjured up images out of their past. Images Dan had tried very hard to banish over the years.

Damn, he was never going to get over her, he thought, resigning himself to his fate.

"Why don't we grab some coffee later when you get your lunch break?" Dan suggested to her. "You seem a little busy now."

The phone was ringing again. "You think?" she asked, reaching for the receiver as she pushed her hair out of her eyes.

"What time's lunch?" he asked. He didn't want to turn up early and have Annie think that he was hovering.

She only had enough time to answer, "Twelve thirty," before she picked up the receiver. "Brooks Smith's Veterinary Clinic, how may I help you?"

The corners of Danny's mouth curved as he walked out of the clinic. At this point, he knew that Jamie had deliberately manipulated him, using the so-called outstanding vet bill as an excuse to get him together with Annie again. He had no more place in her life now than he had earlier this week when he'd gone to see her, but he had to admit that it was nice getting to see her a second time.

He had no idea how much longer he was going to be in Rust Creek Falls—technically, he'd taken only a month's leave of absence from his job to come out here, but he could always leave earlier.

He could also stay longer, he told himself.

It all depended on how things wound up arranging themselves, he thought. But that was something he intended to keep to himself, at least for now.

While he waited for twelve thirty to come, Dan decided to explore the town of Rust Creek Falls so he could feel like a native of the area again and not like some clueless tourist finding his way around.

He found himself gravitating to a diner rather than a restaurant. The diner had caught his attention because of its sign out front. It boasted having "the best cup of coffee for thirty miles around" so he decided to put the claim to the test.

Dan didn't know about "best" but the coffee was at least decent enough to merit a second order.

He nursed the second cup while sitting in a small booth next to a window. It was a deliberate choice. The vantage point allowed him to observe the citizens' comings and goings without really being observed himself.

At this point, he wasn't quite ready to re-connect with anyone he might have known back when he lived here. The truth of it was, he wasn't quite up to answering questions that might come his way, either about what he was currently doing or about what had prompted his brothers and him to leave. That was some-thing he wanted to tackle gradually—after he sorted a few things out with Annie.

Starting with her explanation as to why she'd acted so strangely when he'd said he was here with Jamie's monthly payment.

Sipping his coffee, he scanned the entire dinner. There was an old-fashioned clock on the wall just behind the counter. He caught himself staring at it periodically for the next two and a half hours.

It seemed to him that the minute hand dragged itself from one number to the next with all the speed of a turtle whose feet had been dipped in molasses.

He put up with it as long as he could, then finally paid for his coffee, plus a tip, leaving ten dollars on the table and walking out.

Danny debated killing some more time by walking around Rust Creek Falls, but he still didn't want to run into anyone that he might possibly know, so instead, he got into his car.

Driving around downtown, even at a snail's pace, didn't take any time at all. Before he knew it, Danny found himself back in the parking lot across from the vet clinic.

He killed another half hour just sitting in his Jeep. But this was Montana and it was definitely nippy in October. He didn't want to just run his engine, using up gas needlessly. Besides, running an engine and going nowhere seemed almost too much like a metaphor for his life.

When it got too cold for him, he got out of his vehicle and went back to the clinic.

The moment he entered, the difference in temperature hit him immediately. There were far more warm bodies in the reception area now than there had been earlier.

Annie looked swamped.

There were people standing at her desk, looking less than patient, and she had just put the receiver down into its cradle, ending another call.

Even with all this activity going on simultaneously, she immediately looked toward the door the second he walked in.

Was she waiting for him? he wondered.

Nodding at her, Dan took a seat and made himself as comfortable as he could, given the current circumstances. He was prepared to wait as long has he had to. At this point, he felt as if he had earned that cup of coffee with Annie.

"You're early," Annie said to him when she finally had dealt with the three people at her desk and had answered the two more calls that had come in.

"I didn't want to take a chance on missing you before you went to lunch," he told her.

His words drew several interested looks from the people sitting in the waiting area.

Anne looked at the people in the crowded waiting room. "It might be a little later than twelve thirty," she told him.

He shrugged almost philosophically. "I waited this long, what's another half hour or so?"

Annie pressed her lips together, suppressing the words that rose to her lips in response to his comment. This wasn't the time or place to say anything off-the-cuff. She knew that if she did, within less than a heartbeat, she would find herself the unwilling subject of a barrage of gossip.

Rust Creek Falls was a small town and there weren't all that many things going on to spark people's imaginations or to cut through the all-but-numbing boredom that was known to arise periodically.

In the background, Debi, one of the clinic's technicians, had obviously overheard the exchange between Danny and her because the older woman stepped forward now and approached her.

"If you'd like to go out now and get lunch a little earlier," the technician told her, "that's all right. I'll take over the desk while you're gone."

Anne bit her lower lip and looked at the other woman hesitantly. "Don't you have to assist Brooks, Debi?"

The blonde shook her head. "Ellen's doing that. And Kim is with Dr. Wellington, so you'd better take advantage of this very temporary lull before I change my mind or one of the doctors decide they need more than one tech at their side for a procedure," Debi told her.

"But what about you?" Anne wanted to know. "When will you take your lunch?"

"Nathan is coming by later so I'll wait for him. He says he 'wants to talk,'" the woman confided. "I'd really rather stay busy until he gets here."

From his vantage point, Dan had managed to overhear Anne's part of the exchange and lip-read the rest of it. The moment the older technician told Anne to take her lunch early, he was on his feet, crossing to the reception desk.

"Looks like you've been cleared to go," he told her as the other woman stepped away.

Anne felt butterflies fluttering in the pit of her stomach. Why did she feel as if she was about to go out on a first date? She wasn't, for heaven sakes. This wasn't even a date at all. She was just getting a cup of coffee with someone who had once meant a great deal to her.

Someone you had a baby with, the voice in her head reminded her.

With effort, Anne forced a ghost of a smile to her lips as she said, "Just let me get my purse and then I'll be ready."

Taking out her purse from one of the bottom drawers, Anne rose to her feet. She glanced at the phone, willing it to ring.

It didn't.

She had temporarily run out of possible excuses.

"Okay," she told Danny as she came around to the front of the reception desk, "let's get that cup of coffee."

Taking her elbow to help guide her out of the clinic, Dan murmured, "I thought you'd never ask."

The butterflies went into high gear.

Chapter 8

"Where would you like to go?" Dan asked her as they crossed the parking lot to his Jeep.

"Back to the clinic." The words came out before she could think to stop them.

He paused, intense blue eyes meeting blue eyes.

"Really?" Dan asked.

It wasn't his intention to force her to go anywhere with him. Although if he were given a choice, he would have opted to spend a little more time with her. Who knew when the opportunity to do that would arise again—if ever? Because if he *did* decide to go back to Colorado, he knew that he might never get the chance to see Annie again.

"No, not really," Annie admitted, relenting. "I guess I'm just nervous."

That took him aback. "Nervous?" Dan asked incredulously. Grabbing the passenger door, he held it open for her. "Around me?"

That didn't seem to make any sense to him. He could see Annie being angry at him for leaving and even more angry that he hadn't tried to get in touch with her in all this time. But nervous? Why would he make her nervous? They'd hit it off from the very first day all those years ago. They'd been friends from the very beginning and that friendship had eventually blossomed into love. A case of nerves had never been part of that equation.

"This is me. Danny," he reminded her. "You don't have anything to be nervous about around me."

A lot he knew, Anne thought. Just being near him like this made everything inside of her quiver like a bowlful of Jell-O perched on the side of an active volcano.

One would think, she told herself, trying not to press her hand to her abdomen, that after all this time and everything that had happened, she would have gotten over him.

But she hadn't.

All it had taken was seeing him again, watching him walk back into her life, and all the strides she thought she had made toward overcoming her feelings for Danny just curled up like leaves that had dried out in the summer sun and blew away.

"If you say so," Anne murmured under her breath, sitting down in the passenger seat and putting on her seat belt.

About to start the Jeep, Dan left his hand on the key in the ignition and studied her face. "Why would you be nervous around me?"

She'd said too much, Anne thought. But his question needed an answer so she grasped at the first thing that occurred to her.

"Maybe because I don't know you. The Danny Stockton I knew would have never just disappeared without a word and left me hanging, facing each day wondering if *this* was the day you'd come back to me. But you didn't and after a while, I stopped hoping, I stopped waiting. It got to the point that I thought I just imagined all of it, except for…"

Her voice trailed off when she realized she'd almost said *except for Janie*.

But he had obviously heard her. "Except for what?" Dan prodded.

Anne waved away the mistake she'd very nearly made. "Never mind, it doesn't matter," she told him.

"Annie, if you'd really rather I just take you back to the clinic, I will," Dan offered, although not happily. Still, he could understand how she felt and he couldn't really fault her for it. He didn't want to be the cause of any more unhappiness.

Annie looked at him, her expression unreadable. "Do you want me to go back?"

How could she even *think* that? "Hell, no," he answered with feeling. "I know I can't begin to make up for what happened, for just disappearing the way I did. All I can tell you is that I had a good reason and you're just going to have to trust me. And if you can find it in your heart to forgive me," he told her in all sincerity, "I'd really love to spend a little time with you."

He knew he had no right to even ask that, but just being here with her like this made his soul sing.

"*Little* is certainly the word for it," she answered. "I've only got an hour for lunch."

An hour was more than he would have hoped for. "It's a start," Dan told her, relieved that she had decided to have lunch with him. "So, where do you want to go to eat?" he asked again.

An amused smile played on her lips. "Maybe you haven't noticed, but Rust Creek Falls is not exactly brimming with restaurants." She thought for a moment. "Daisy's Donut Shop serves coffee and the pastries are really good."

That didn't make for much of a lunch, but if that was what she wanted, that was where he'd take her. "Any place you want to go is fine with me," Dan told her. "Or we could order something to go," he suggested.

She thought the idea was to sit and talk over the meal. "You don't want to be seen with me?" Anne asked.

Where would she get an idea like that? He was just trying to be accommodating. Maybe he was trying too hard, he thought.

"I was just thinking that you might not want to be seen with *me*," he told her. Granted, she was divorced, but that wouldn't stop tongues from wagging in Rust Creek Falls. "I was afraid that you might be worried that it could start some gossip."

Annie shrugged. Gossip had never bothered her. "I'm single, you're single—" She stopped, wondering if she was perhaps taking too much for granted. "You *are* single, right?"

"Very," he answered. There'd never been another woman who had made him feel the way he did about her. He didn't see the point in just marrying someone for the sake of being married.

But Anne wasn't totally convinced about his status. "There's no one back in Colorado waiting for you? A 'Miss Dude Ranch' maybe?"

"Not in Colorado or anywhere else, either," Danny assured her.

Danny had always been the handsomest guy that she had ever laid eyes on. She knew what women were like—he'd be a trophy for anyone who landed him.

"So you've been a monk all this time?" she asked with just the slightest touch of sarcasm in her voice.

His face was completely straight as he told her, "Pretty much."

She gave him one last chance to come clean. "With those muscles and those brilliant blue eyes?" She knew that they had been her undoing and thought that they would easily do the same for another woman.

Danny's eyes looked into hers. "Yup."

Annie still had her doubts, but for now, she went along with his answer. She tried to hang on to the fact that Danny had never lied to her.

"Okay, then there's nothing to gossip about," she concluded. "Just two single people having coffee."

Taking that to be the end of the discussion, he drove to Daisy's Donut Shop.

The donut shop was crowded when they got there. It turned out to be standing room only by the admittedly small counter.

"Looks like we're going to have to get that coffee to go anyway," Dan told her. She nodded and for a moment, he could have sworn that Annie actually looked a little disappointed. He found that encouraging. "We could go to Wings To Go instead," he suggested.

They might be able to grab a little table there, Danny thought.

The look on Annie's face reflected confusion. "I thought you wanted coffee."

"What I wanted," he told her truthfully, "was just to spend a little time with you. The coffee was actually just an excuse."

"All right, then. We're having wings," Annie agreed.

He was getting to her, she thought, but as long as they were out in public, she had nothing to worry about.

Wings To Go was a cozy little restaurant that, in Dan's estimation, showed a lot of potential. He could see investors making a lot of money here if they expanded the place. Right now it was packed, so he ordered two plates of wings and two soft drinks to go, one for each of them, along with a ton of napkins, and took them back to his Jeep.

"I guess this is kind of like a picnic," he told her. Danny pushed back his seat so that he had enough room to spread out several napkins and balance his box of wings on his lap.

"Remember the one we had on your family's ranch?" Annie asked, instantly stirring up a whole bunch of memories.

"I remember that the stars were out by the time we finished eating," Dan recalled.

More than that, he remembered every detail of that night. It had been the closest thing to perfect he had ever experienced.

That was the night we made a baby, Anne thought.

When his eyes met hers, she knew that Danny was remembering the same thing. Not the baby part, because he had no way of knowing she'd gotten pregnant. Instead he was remembering that had been the night when they'd made love for the first—and the last—time. A week after that, his parents were in that awful car accident. And then, right after the funeral, he was gone.

The mention of the picnic not only brought a flood of memories back for Danny, but it also made him feel utterly drawn to her.

There they were, in his Jeep, two orders of buffalo wings spread out between them and all he could think of was taking her into his arms and kissing her.

That would be all she'd need, he upbraided himself, to have him force unwanted attention on her. Desperate to change the subject, he searched for something else to say and remembered the look on her face when he'd explained why he had walked into the clinic.

Like a drowning man grasping at straws, he asked Annie, "Um, why did you look so confused when I told you that Jamie wanted me to bring in his monthly payment to the clinic?"

Stunned, Annie blinked. The subject had changed so fast, she'd almost gotten whiplash. For a second there, Danny had had that look in his eyes, that same look he'd had that night at the picnic.

She'd thought he was going to kiss her.

Idiot! she chided herself. She couldn't allow him to kiss her. That would be starting something that *couldn't* be started.

At least one of them had some sense.

She forced herself to think back to this morning. "Um, because Jamie doesn't have an outstanding balance with the vet. Your brother makes a point of paying each time the vet comes out to the ranch."

That was the impression he'd gotten when she'd appeared so confused and surprised this morning. "So what was in the envelope when you finally opened it?" he wanted to know.

"Oh, there was a check in there," she told him. "It was for a small amount. And he included a note. He said it was an advance against the vet's next visit."

"I guess he was trying to come up with an excuse to get me to see you again," Dan said, feeling somewhat self-conscious.

He didn't like being manipulated, but at the same time, he understood why Jamie had done it. His brother's heart was in the right place. Having found happiness, Jamie no doubt wanted the same for him.

Not going to happen, Jamie.

"Yes, I kind of figured that part out," Annie told him with a self-deprecating laugh.

"And I would like to see you again," Dan told her.

Finished eating, she wiped her fingers on one of the many napkins Danny had thought to bring with the take-out orders. "You mean for lunch?"

Danny shrugged, not wanting to restrict himself with anything so specific. "For lunch. For a walk. Or maybe we could go horseback riding the way we used to," he reminded her. Danny saw the uncertain expression slip over her face. Maybe that was too much, he thought as he backtracked. "Or just to talk."

"About what?"

"We don't need to have a topic outlined ahead of time," he reminded her. "We can talk about whatever comes up." And then he went another route. "Or we don't need to talk at all. We can just enjoy each other's company." Finished with his lunch, he packed the wrappers back up into the box and folded it over to contain the denuded bones and used napkins. "Tell you what. I'll come by Daisy's Donut Shop tomorrow at twelve thirty. If you want to join me, that'll be great. If you decide that you don't want to, or you have second thoughts, I'll understand." His eyes met hers. "No pressure," he promised softly.

Danny's magnetic blue eyes had always had a way of getting to her. She could recall getting happily lost in them for hours.

"Twelve thirty," Annie repeated. And then she glanced down at her watch. "Oh damn," she said, clearly distressed. Before he could ask her what was wrong, she told him. "I'm late. I'm supposed to be back in the office. I went to lunch early, remember?"

He did now. Time had stood still for him as he'd reveled in her company, but she was right. The hour she'd had was gone.

"I'll tell your boss it was my fault," he volunteered as he started the Jeep and pulled away. "I made you late."

She appreciated what he was offering to do, but it wasn't necessary.

"No, that's all right. I'm a grown woman, Danny. Nobody 'makes' me anything. I've been working for the doctor for a while now. I'll just tell him that I lost track of time and I'll promise to make it up by coming in early tomorrow. Brooks is a good guy. He'll understand."

Danny was skeptical. "Are you sure? I don't mind talking to him and taking the blame."

"No," she said firmly. There was no way she wanted to have someone make excuses for her, least of all Danny.

He was silent for a moment. "I didn't mean to make you late."

Having him feel guilty about something so minor was not the way to go if their relationship had any hopes of being repaired. There were far bigger issues that still needed to be resolved, not the least of which was whether or not to tell Danny the truth about Janie's parentage.

She also sensed that there was something he wasn't telling her, and until he could trust her enough to level with her, their relationship was going to be in a suspended state.

"You didn't know what time I was supposed to get back. It's up to me to keep track of the time," she informed him.

He laughed softly. "I guess motherhood really changed you."

He meant it as a compliment, but he had a feeling from her answer that Annie didn't quite take it that way.

"Twelve years changed me," she corrected. "I was a teenager when you left Rust Creek Falls. I'm not a teenager anymore."

He came to a stop right in front of the clinic rather than in the parking lot across the way. His eyes washed over her, as if seeing her for the first time since he'd arrived back.

"No," he replied, "you're not."

There was notable appreciation in Danny's voice that was not lost on her. She felt a warmth climbing up along her throat, leaving its mark on her cheeks.

Annie felt it best not to say anything in response to his comment. Instead, she got out of the Jeep.

"Thanks for lunch," she said just before she ran through the clinic's front door.

Without being able to explain exactly why, Dan felt as if he'd been on the receiving end of a one-two punch. Blowing out a breath, he pulled away and drove back to Jamie's ranch.

Dan looked at his watch.

It was thirty seconds later than it had been when he'd looked at his watch the last time. Twelve thirty had come and gone and one o'clock was looming on the horizon, just ninety seconds away.

He was sitting in Daisy's Donut Shop.

Alone.

Annie hadn't come.

He thought—again—of calling the vet clinic to speak to her. He'd already thought of doing that twice before and each time, he'd wound up talking himself out of it. He didn't want to make Annie feel like he was bothering her at work or even worse, that he was stalking her.

Most likely, she had gotten swamped at the clinic again the way she had yesterday. Or maybe one of the vet techs had called in sick and there was no one to man the reception desk when she went to lunch.

Or, for that matter, maybe she had just changed her mind and decided that seeing him again—especially seeing him two days in a row—was a bad idea. Undoubtedly Annie was just going to work through her lunch and completely forget about seeing him today.

Or possibly ever.

If that was the case, Annie was definitely within her rights, he thought. For that matter, she might even view this as payback for what she felt he had done to her by taking off the way he had right after his parents' funeral.

Thinking back to that day, he recalled that she'd held his hand all through it, squeezing it the way people did when they were trying to infuse their own strength into someone else, hoping to help them get through something particularly devastating.

Annie had really tried to help him get through that difficult time, doing the best she could—and he had still left her.

Danny sighed. Annie wasn't coming, he realized, resigning himself to the fact.

Very slowly, he got up, easing himself away

from the tiny table for two. His appetite gone, he left the coffee and donuts he'd bought in anticipation of her company and headed for the door.

Just as he was about to push open the door in order to go out, the door was suddenly moved out of range. Hand outstretched, he found himself tripping forward.

Chapter 9

Danny managed to catch himself a second before he made bodily contact with the customer who was entering the donut shop at that exact moment.

Annie swallowed a gasp. Instinct took over and rather than stepping back out of harm's way, her hands flew out to him, anticipating his fall.

Her heart was pounding wildly in her chest as she asked him, "Are you okay?"

Dan caught himself grinning like a kid who'd stumbled across Christmas presents in the closet in October.

"You came," he exclaimed. "I'm terrific."

Anne stepped inside the coffee shop to get out of people's way.

"You were leaving, weren't you?" It wasn't a question; it was an assumption. She flushed just a tad. Her heart slowly began to settle down. "I'm sorry I'm so late, but things went a little crazy at the clinic."

Dan nodded understandingly. "I figured as much," he told her. Now that Annie was here, he didn't want her to waste any time with needless apologies. "I ordered for us. I'm afraid the coffee's probably cold, but the pastries are still fresh."

Annie smiled. "No problem. I love cold coffee."

She said it so that Danny wouldn't feel bad, but the truth of it was she really did like coffee no matter what state it was in.

Placing his hand against the small of her back, he steered Annie toward the little table he'd just occupied for the last forty-five minutes.

As he approached, he saw that one of the people from behind the counter was beginning to clear away the coffees and pastries.

"No, hey, wait," he called out to the woman, "I wasn't done with that."

The waitress immediately deposited the dishes of pastries back onto the table. "Oh, I'm sorry, I thought I saw you leaving."

"No, I was just going to get a little air." He pretended to inhale. "You've got great air here in Montana. Crisp and clean."

The waitress looked at him as if he'd taken leave of his senses.

"It's cold," was all she would say about it. Putting the closed containers of coffee back on the table, the woman withdrew.

As she did, she gave Annie a warning look. "I'd watch myself around him if I were you."

"I fully intend to," Annie answered with a smile, looking at Danny and not the waitress. "Do you want to take those somewhere and eat?" she asked him, thinking that he would probably like to get out of the little shop.

"No, she's right. Montana's cold. You don't want to spend your lunch hour sitting in a Jeep, shivering." He pulled out her chair for her, then took his own after taking off his jacket and draping it on the back of the chair. "So," he started, amicably, giving her his full attention, "what happened?"

"What happened?" she echoed, not quite sure what he was asking her about.

"To make you late," he prodded.

Annie waved his question away. It was just the usual work stuff, compounded. She had no desire to bore him to death.

"Oh, you don't want to hear about my morning."

"Sure I do," he told her with feeling. "It's got to be more interesting than standing outside in the cold, fixing twenty feet of fencing."

"Well," she allowed, "I guess it was warmer at any rate."

He smiled at Annie, watching the way the rays of sun played off her hair, turning the blond strands into gold. "Sounds more interesting already."

Annie's expression was somewhat dubious as she looked at him. "All right," she agreed, "but remember, you asked for this."

"You won't hear one single word of complaint," he promised, making an elaborate show of crossing his heart with the hand that wasn't holding a cream-filled chocolate donut.

Annie laughed and the sound was like music to his ears.

* * *

The next fifty minutes passed much too quickly. Annie did most of the talking and it was as if they had regained some of their former relationship, at least a little of the ease that they had once felt around one another.

And then, just as she finished the last of her pastry, he told her, "You'd better be getting back." Annie looked at him, puzzled. "Your lunch break is almost over," he explained.

"You're keeping track?" she asked, surprised. She hadn't seen him look down at his watch.

He nodded. "I didn't want you to be late two days in a row," he told her, rising and coming around behind her chair. He held it as he helped her out of it.

Bemused, Annie asked, "You actually timed this?"

He couldn't tell if she was amused or offended by his action. All he could do was restate his reason. "Like I said, I didn't want you to be late getting back again because of me."

As they walked out of the shop, Danny held the door open for her. She smiled at him as she crossed the threshold.

"What?" he asked. He needed to know why she was smiling so he could do whatever it was again. "Do I have some cream filling on my face?"

Annie shook her head. "No."

"Then why are you looking at me that way?" he wanted to know.

"It's nice to know that there's a little of the old Danny still left inside you."

There were times when he really doubted that, even though he had done his best not to let what had happened—what he had *caused* to happen—bury him in despair. "What makes you say that?"

"Because someone else would not have gone through the trouble of keeping track of the time, or worrying about me being late getting back to work." There was a fond look in her eyes as she said, "But the old Danny would have. And you did."

They were by her car now and Dan realized this was the last moment he was going to spend with her for at least a while. A feeling of sadness corkscrewed through him.

"Terminal nice guy, that's me," Danny responded with just a touch of sarcasm.

She saw that the sadness in his eyes that

had been missing for a little while as they'd talked in the donut shop was back. She wanted to erase it even though she told herself it shouldn't matter to her one way or another.

"Nothing wrong with being a nice guy," she told him softly.

He made no comment. Instead, he told her, "This was nice. Maybe we can do it again sometime."

She noticed that he didn't say anything definite the way he had yesterday. Was he afraid of committing himself to something specific?

"I'd like that," Annie told him. "But right now, I have to go."

"Right."

Dan stepped back, although in reality, he wasn't blocking her from her car. Annie's vehicle was right behind her, a ten-year-old pickup truck whose paint was fading in several places. The step back he'd taken was more symbolic than actually necessary. He didn't want to seem as if he was trying to detain her for even an extra minute.

"I'll see you, Annie," he said as she got into her truck.

"I hope so," she answered just before she started up her vehicle and pulled away.

Danny lost no time in getting into his Jeep. He'd told Jamie he'd be back in plenty of time to help him fix the north gate. He intended to keep his word.

I hope so.

The words echoed in his head all the way back to Jamie's. It accompanied the smile that was on his face.

"So things are going well?" Jamie asked, eyeing Dan over the gate that they were trying to put back up after they'd mended it.

Jamie had waited to ask his question for what he thought was a decent amount of time after Danny had gotten back from town. He was proud of himself for not immediately jumping on his brother to pump Danny for information.

"Yeah, I just about got this gate straight," Danny answered, grunting for effect.

"I'm not talking about the stupid gate," Jamie said in exasperation.

Waiting until he had hammered the three nails he'd been holding in his teeth to the two sides of the gate, Dan looked at his brother with mock innocence and asked, "Then what are you talking about?"

Jamie scowled. "You know damn well what I'm talking about, Danny. Those trips of yours into town."

"Oh yeah. I'm really beginning to find my way around town again."

Jamie thought he'd been patient long enough.

"I'm holding a hammer, Danny," he told him, grasping the tool harder, "and I know how to use it."

Danny gave him a look as he held up his hammer. "That makes two of us, brother," he answered.

"So she shut you out?" Jamie asked, assuming the only thing he could since Danny wasn't saying that things had gone at least moderately well. "Hey, Danny, I'm sorry. Maybe it just wasn't meant to—"

"You want to work or you want to gossip?" Danny wanted to know.

"What I want is to work and to have a conversation with my brother while I'm working," Jamie answered.

Danny sighed. He supposed he owed Jamie this much. "It's going well enough. There, you satisfied?" he asked, looking at Jamie pointedly.

Jamie was light years away from being satisfied. "What do you mean by 'well enough'?"

Danny sighed again. "You're worse than Old Mrs. McKinley, you know that?" The woman their mother had known years ago had loved to gossip and to ferret out information about people. Some people had felt that it was her whole life.

Jamie looked annoyed by the comparison. "You're my brother. Forgive me for caring," he retorted.

Danny pressed his lips together, debating what to do. He knew he was being secretive about something that was most likely general public knowledge, at least to anyone who lived in town.

"I'm sorry. It's just that I'm afraid if I say anything at all about it, then it will no longer be the truth."

Jamie saw through the flimsy excuse. "You mean you're afraid of jinxing it."

The game was up. Danny felt he might as well relent. "Something like that."

"Since when did you get so superstitious?" Jamie wanted to know.

"I didn't realize I was until just now," Danny admitted. "And to answer your question, it's been going well enough." He paused, searching for something more to give Jamie. There really wasn't anything. "Baby steps," he finally told his brother. "The whole thing is progressing with baby steps."

Jamie nodded. "Sounds hopeful."

"Yeah, maybe," Danny allowed. He didn't want to say anything more about it at the moment. To him, the whole thing was very fragile in nature and he didn't want to count on it too much one way or another. "Now if you want to finish this gate before the triplets are ready to start high school, I suggest you talk less and work more."

Jamie laughed. Now *that* sounded like the old Danny. "Welcome back, brother."

Danny merely grunted as he hammered.

"Is that guy your old boyfriend?" Janie asked that evening as she was helping her mother clear the table after they'd had dinner.

The question had come out of nowhere and caught Anne totally off guard. Gathering up the utensils from the table, she forced herself to make eye contact with her daughter.

"Who are you talking about?" she asked,

although she knew full well there could only be one person that Janie was referring to.

Janie gave her an impatient look that pre-teen daughters had been giving their mothers since the very beginning of time.

"That guy that came to see you last week before Dad came to pick me up."

Rather than give Janie an answer, she deflected with a question of her own. "Just what makes you ask something like that?"

Janie pursed her lips together as if the answer was self-evident. "You had a funny look on your face when you were talking to him."

"I was just surprised to see him," Anne said, thinking fast. "He hasn't been in Rust Creek Falls for a long time."

"Then he wasn't your old boyfriend?" Janie asked, clearly wanting an answer one way or another.

Anne turned to load the dishwasher. She didn't want to lie to her daughter, but she really didn't want to get into this at the present time. "Why do you want to know?"

Janie gave her an annoyed look. "Because I want you and Dad to get back together and you can't do that if your old boyfriend is hanging around, getting you all dreamy-eyed and stuff," she said in disgust.

"Honey, your dad and I aren't going to get back together," Anne said, repeating what she'd already told her daughter more than once. "But we still both love you very much. As for Danny, I knew him a long time ago. Before I met your father," she added. "Do you like him?"

Janie shrugged. "He's okay I guess. For an old guy."

Ouch, that stung, Anne thought. "He's the same age as I am," she pointed out to her daughter.

"Yeah, but you're old, too," Janie said as she brought over the plates to the kitchen counter. "Not frumpy old," she quickly corrected. "But old."

Anne smiled. She couldn't ever remember being as young as Janie. Had she said things like this at the time? She certainly hoped not.

Very tactfully, she told Janie, "Sometimes 'old' people like to see old friends."

"Dad's old," Janie pointed out, brightening. "You can see *him*."

"I do see him," Anne replied. "When he

comes by to pick you up and on the following day, when he drops you off."

Janie's scowl deepened. "I mean *more*, Mom," she stressed. "Like you used to see him. All the time."

Anne sighed. She knew this mode. Janie was just going to keep on harping on the subject until she either broke Anne down, or she lost her temper. Anne didn't want to do either.

She fell back on her old standby. "Have you finished your homework for tomorrow?"

"Not yet, but—"

"Then go finish it," Anne told her, cutting through any more rhetoric.

"But this is *important*, Mom," Janie insisted, becoming irritated.

Finished loading the dishwasher, Anne measured out the detergent, put it into the proper compartment and started the cycle.

"So's your homework," she declared. "If you don't do it, you'll get left back and that'll throw everything off. How will it look when you're running for president and your opponent finds out you were left back in fifth grade?"

Janie sighed dramatically. It was audible

over the noise of the dishwasher. "I'm not going to run for president, Mom."

"You need to pass fifth grade no matter what you intend on doing in life," she told her daughter matter-of-factly.

"Okay, I'll do it, I'll do it," Janie declared, putting her hands over her ears to shut out any further pep talk from her mother. "I'll do my homework so I don't flunk out of fifth grade."

"That's my girl," Anne said with a smile. She went back to cleaning up the kitchen.

"This isn't over, you know," Janie promised as she left the kitchen.

Anne shut her eyes as she leaned her head against the wall, struggling very hard to collect herself.

Yes, I know, she said silently.

It wasn't going to be over until she made a full confession—to both Janie and to Danny.

Chapter 10

There was no word from Danny the next day. Annie tried to pretend that she didn't care one way or another. That she was relieved not to have to deal with having Danny coming around. But the truth was that not hearing from him had her concerned and wondering if something had gone wrong.

Again.

Had he decided to go back to that dude ranch in Colorado, the one he said he worked on? Or had he decided, after seeing her twice, that he was making a huge mistake starting things up again? That he was actually open-

ing up a can of worms that was best left un-
opened and buried somewhere back in the
distant past?

It was the not knowing that was putting
her on edge, so much so that she found people were talking to her twice because she'd
drifted off.

It was happening, she realized. She was letting Danny get to her, just as she had let his
disappearance get to her twelve years ago.

*C'mon, Anne, you're better than this.
You're not a teenager anymore. You're a
grown woman and a mother with responsi-
bilities. Your world isn't supposed to revolve
around whether or not Danny Stockton turns
up on your doorstep.*

She forced herself to focus on her work
and remained at the reception desk, working
straight through her lunch break.

But no matter what she told herself, all
that day it felt like every fiber of her being
kept waiting for Danny to turn up, first at the
clinic and then later, at her home.

He didn't.

By the middle of the second day, she'd almost convinced herself that Dan Stockton had

gone from her life just as abruptly as he had turned up.

Now she just had to make her peace with it. She told herself she could—but it was far from easy. So far that when Hank came by her house later that afternoon to pick Janie up for an overnight stay, he asked her, "Something wrong, Anne?"

"Nothing more than usual," she answered evasively. "They were shorthanded at the clinic today, and between the house calls the vets had to make to the different ranches and the pets people brought in themselves, things have been pretty hectic all week."

She noticed Hank peered closely at her face and figured she was in trouble. She'd never been one to maintain a poker face. "That the only thing bothering you?" he wanted to know.

She tossed her head as she looked up, doing her best to bluff her way through this. "Why? What else would there be?"

She could both feel and see Hank studying her. It was all she could do not to shift uncomfortably.

"Maybe an old flame turning up without any warning," he suggested.

Rather than deny anything, she decided to brazen it out and hopefully make Hank back off. "That's not really any of your concern, Hank."

But Hank obviously saw it another way. "Yes, it is. Daniel Stockton ran out on you when you needed him most," he insisted angrily.

"Stop!"

She didn't want Hank saying anything about Danny that Janie could accidentally overhear. She wasn't ready to tell her daughter about the circumstances of her birth and she certainly didn't want the girl to find out by hearing Hank talking about it.

"That's all in the past," she informed him sternly. "And as far as I'm concerned, that's exactly where it belongs."

But the expression on his face told her that Hank was far from convinced. "Are you sure, Anne?"

She moved closer to him, but not out of any desire to rekindle something between them. There had never been anything between them except for respect and gratitude on her part. But she didn't want what she was about to say to Hank to be overheard.

"As far as Janie knows, you're her father and she's always going to think of you that way." She lowered her voice even more as she added, "You've got nothing to worry about."

He looked relieved to hear her say that. "I love that little girl, Anne," he told her, emotion brimming in his voice.

"I know, Hank, and she loves you. That's never going to change."

He looked over Anne's shoulder as Janie came into the room, backpack in tow. His whole countenance changed, lightening up right before her.

"Well, speak of the devil," he declared in a louder, more jovial voice.

"I'm not the devil, Dad," Janie protested as she came over to join him.

"Well, sometimes you act like a little devil," Hank teased affectionately.

They had a good relationship, Anne observed. She couldn't remember Hank ever raising his voice or saying a cross word to Janie. She found herself almost wishing that Hank really *was* Janie's father. Things would have been a lot simpler that way.

"I'm all ready to go, Dad," Janie announced, impatient to leave.

Hank took her backpack from her and pretended that he found it extremely heavy. Suppressing a grunt, he said, "I can see that."

"Be good and listen to your dad," Anne instructed her daughter.

Janie rolled her eyes. "Yes, Mom." Turning to Hank, she confided, "She thinks I'm a baby."

"You'll always be my baby," Anne interjected, deliberately giving the girl a big hug.

Janie groaned and squirmed, acting as if she was being subjected to corporal punishment. The second Anne released her, Janie deliberately moved out of her mother's reach.

Pretending not to notice and giving no indication that it hurt, Anne walked Hank and her daughter to the door.

"Have fun, you two," she told them.

"Oh, we will," Hank promised, saying the words more to Janie than to her. "Tell your mother goodbye," he told the girl.

"Bye," Janie said without bothering to look back in her mother's direction. She was too eager to begin whatever adventure her father had planned for them.

As was her habit, Anne watched them go. Watched how her daughter skipped beside

Hank, the picture of uncomplicated happiness—and the total antithesis of the way she usually behaved when it was just the two of them, without Hank.

Janie's change in behavior had been recent, no more than about three, four months old. It was around that time that Janie had gotten it into her head to play Cupid and bring Hank and her together. Anne had explained to her daughter a number of times, in as many ways as she could think of, that sometimes parents just couldn't stay together and that it was far better for all parties involved if parents weren't forced to live together. But that never seemed to stick in Janie's mind for more than a few minutes at a time. It certainly wasn't anything that Janie took to heart.

Anne saw Hank say something to Janie as she got into his car and the child laughed in response.

Anne sighed as she closed the door. She wished that Janie could be that happy around her.

It hadn't always been like this, she recalled. When it had been the three of them together, Janie had always turned to her first. But ever since the divorce, Hank had slowly become her daughter's go-to person.

Anne frowned. She supposed she was being a little jealous of Hank. That was something she was going to have to work on. It wasn't right to feel like that about someone who was so good to—

Her thought pulled up short when she heard the doorbell.

Anne laughed softly to herself. Janie had probably remembered she hadn't packed one of her video games.

Opening the door, she asked, "Forget something?"

"Yeah. My manners."

It wasn't her daughter but Danny standing on her doorstep, just as he had the first time he'd turned up in Rust Creek Falls several days ago.

Damn, was her heart ever going to stop leaping up this way at the very sight of him? Anne wondered, annoyed with herself.

Forcing a smile to her lips, she said, "I hear there's a current shortage of that." Then she stepped back from the doorway to let him come in.

Dan crossed the threshold, but went no further into the room. He looked just a touch apprehensive. "Am I interrupting anything?" he asked hesitantly.

"Only my solitude," she answered truthfully. "Janie just left for a sleepover at Hank's and I was about to go over some bills I've been letting pile up."

"So in other words, no?" he asked, an engaging smile on his lips. He looked very happy with her answer.

Anne inclined her head. "In other words, no," she repeated. "Would you like to come in?" she asked, assuming that was why he was here.

"Actually, I was wondering if you'd like to come out," he told her.

She suddenly realized that the carefree girl who would take off at a moment's notice at the slightest suggestion from Danny was gone. Instead, she heard herself asking, "Come out where?"

"I was going to ask if you and Janie would like to go horseback riding with me, but since you just said that she's not here, I'm asking if *you'd* like to go for a ride with me."

"Now?" she asked, looking outside over his shoulder. "Isn't it going to be dark soon?"

"I was thinking of going out for only a short ride," he explained. "But if you'd rather not, we can do it some other time."

Temptation won after what turned out to be an extremely short internal debate.

"Sure, why not?" Anne agreed. "As long as it's a short ride," she qualified. "Give me a minute."

Getting her jacket and keys, Anne stepped out onto her porch and looked around. She didn't see what she was looking for.

"Where are you keeping the horses?" she asked in amusement, fully expecting him to tell her that he'd only been teasing her.

Instead, Danny said, "C'mon and I'll take you to them."

Her curiosity definitely aroused, Anne climbed into his Jeep.

Dan drove only a short distance until he arrived at a stable located not that far out of town. Anne hadn't even known of its existence.

The scope of her world had shrunk a great deal since she'd come back to Rust Creek Falls after college, she thought.

"I thought you might like to go for a horse-back ride," Dan told her, "just like we used to when we were young."

There were five stalls inside the stable. Three were empty. The other two had horses that were already saddled. She thought that was rather unusual, but made no comment about it.

"Which one's mine?" Anne asked. She was instinctively drawn to the smaller mount.

Dan nodded toward the horse that was closer to her. "The mare."

It was a Palomino and she thought the horse was absolutely gorgeous. But something wasn't right. "There are only two saddled horses," she noted, turning to face Dan. "I thought you said that you were inviting Janie, too."

"I had a feeling you'd say no to that if she was home. Besides, I took a chance that her father might have picked her up for the evening," he confessed. "Turns out I was right." Taking both horses out of their stalls, he led them outside the stable. "Ready?"

"Ready," she answered.

Dan handed her the reins to her horse and Anne happily swung into the mare's saddle. She hadn't ridden in years. Not since she and Hank had been divorced. Once they had gone their separate ways, her access to horses and even to a ranch became a thing of the past. Although Janie still got to ride whenever she stayed over at Hank's ranch.

Hank had bought her a pony for her fifth birthday, just shortly before the decision to get a divorce had been made. The pony, Anne suspected, was Hank's way to ensure that Janie would want to come over and spend time with him.

As if he needed to bribe Janie, Anne thought. The girl worshipped the ground he walked on.

Less than five minutes into the ride and it was as if she had never been off a horse. Anne was exhilarated and revitalized.

Urging her mount into first a brisk walk, then a canter and finally a full gallop, she laughed with glee as the seductive feeling of freedom she always experienced on horse-back surged through her veins.

Dan was quietly relieved that she wasn't asking any questions about where the horses had come from. He didn't want her to know he'd arranged for Jamie to bring them over in his trailer to what was essentially an abandoned stable, and to get them saddled.

The look on Anne's face made all this worth it, Dan thought.

He let her set the pace and kept up, happy just to see her like this, with the wind in her hair and nipping at her cheeks, turning them an enticing shade of pink.

The ride was over all too soon. Daylight was beginning to fade. It would be dark before long. Dan called out, "We'd better head back."

Like a gleeful child, Anne wanted to ask for five more minutes. But at the last moment, she stopped herself. He was right. She couldn't just ride off into the night the way she used to.

For one thing, they weren't on Dan's family ranch and she didn't know her way around. For another, she wasn't the girl she'd once been. Freedom in this case belonged to the very young. She'd had her taste of it, but now it was time to go back home.

They brought the horses back to the stable and returned them to their stalls.

"Shouldn't we take their saddles off?" she asked. She didn't see anyone in the stable to take care of the animals.

"That's taken care of," he told her, not

going into details. "Come on, I'll bring you back to your place."

Perplexed, Anne got into his Jeep, then waited until he had pulled the vehicle away and was heading to her house before she told him, "Thank you. That was really fun. I've forgotten what it was like to have fun," she confessed.

"You should always be able to have fun," he told her with sincerity.

She looked at his profile, wondering if he actually meant what he'd just said. And if he did, then why had he ever left her?

Oh, she understood the basic reason that had supposedly compelled him as well as his older brothers to leave town. She knew all about his grandparents and their unwillingness to take in any of the Stockton siblings, much less the three older boys who were legally old enough to be out on their own.

But if Dan meant what he'd just said, *really* meant it, and if he'd really loved her the way he'd told her that wonderful night they'd spent beneath the stars, then why had he left her? Why hadn't he found some way for them to remain together?

That question had been eating away at her for twelve years.

"Why'd you leave me, Danny?" she asked quietly.

"I told you why. You already know the answer to that."

"No, I don't. Not really," she said, then placed her hand over her heart. "Not in here."

He pulled up in front of her house. "You want me to go?" he asked.

"No, I want you to come inside and talk to me. Really talk to me," she told him. She felt that he needed to give her an explanation, a *real* explanation, just as much as she needed to hear one.

Turning off the ignition, he began to get out of the vehicle, but then he wavered. "Maybe I'd better not," he began.

But Annie had anticipated Danny's possible change of heart and she felt that she had gone too far out on that limb to allow him to make his way back to where it was safe.

To where he could act as if their last night together—their only night together—hadn't happened. Because it definitely had. Janie was living proof that it had.

She took hold of Danny's hand and tugged on it, drawing him to her doorstep.

"Maybe you should," she coaxed. "Remember," she told him as she unlocked her door and held it open, "confession is good for the soul."

"That only works if you still have a soul," he qualified.

"Everybody has a soul, Danny." Anne closed the front door behind them and then locked it.

"No," Dan contradicted. "Everyone starts out with a soul. That doesn't mean that they still have it as time goes by."

Anne had no idea what he was talking about. All she knew was that something was apparently haunting Danny and she was convinced that he needed to get it off his chest in order to get better.

Chapter 11

He needed to talk to her.

It was obvious that he had demons, despite his outward facade.

"Would you like a drink?" she offered. Whenever Hank had been tense about something in the past, he always said that a little scotch and soda could always make him feel calmer.

The mere mention of a drink brought that awful night back to Dan in vivid, chilling terms. He could almost feel the hairs on the back of his neck standing up.

"Danny, what's wrong?" Anne asked, reacting to the way the color had drained from his face. "You just turned pale."

It was a mistake coming inside, he told himself. He needed to get away.

"Maybe I'm coming down with something. I should go." He turned toward the door. "I don't want to risk you catching anything from me."

But Annie caught his hand in hers. He found her grip to be surprisingly strong.

"You're not coming down with something," she told him knowingly. "Danny, trust me. Please," she implored. "You have to tell me what's eating away at you, what kept you away from me all these years."

He fell back on his old standby. It was, after all, true. "I left because my grandparents didn't want me. You know that."

Anne's gut told her that wasn't true. "You didn't leave because of your grandparents. You left because something was wrong. I sensed it at your parents' funeral. Just talk to me," she pleaded. "You can't keep running from whatever this is for the rest of your life."

There was no reason to burden her with this. It was his cross to carry, not hers.

"There's no point in talking about it. I

didn't deserve you then, and I don't deserve you now." It was crazy for him to have thought things could be different from what they were. "I should have never come back to Rust Creek Falls."

"Don't tell me what I deserve or don't deserve," she told him angrily. "I'm the only one who can be the judge of that. And in order to be the judge, I need to know what's at the bottom of all this." Her eyes held his as she begged, "Talk to me, Danny. You owe me that much. If I ever meant anything at all to you, you owe me that."

Danny sighed as he stared up at the ceiling, searching for the right words to tell her about this awful segment of his life.

There were no "right" ones, he realized. There were only the ones that described what had happened and what he did that brought about the horrific chain of events. Words that he had kept locked up inside of him for more than a decade. Words he'd never shared with anyone, not even his brothers.

Words that weighed so heavily on him that right now he felt close to the breaking point.

"Please," Anne whispered, squeezing his hand, her eyes silently pleading with him to tell her what had taken him away from her and what was still ripping him apart this way.

Telling himself she was right, that he had to try to tell Annie about it, Dan took a breath and began talking.

"The night of the accident, I went out with Luke and Bailey. They said they wanted to celebrate—I don't even remember what it was that they wanted to celebrate," he said. That memory had gotten lost. "But I didn't realize they were talking about drinking until we walked into a bar.

"Even so," he continued, "I thought they were just going to have one or two drinks. But that turned into more and before I knew it, they were both drunk. Only Luke was old enough to legally drink," he confided, "but Bailey had a fake ID. I asked them to stop, but they told me I was a mama's boy and I needed to 'man up.'"

"Did you drink?" Anne asked.

"No. They taunted me a little, but I knew it was just the alcohol talking. Pretty soon, they were too drunk to drive home and I knew that if *I* tried to drive them home, they'd both gang up on me and never let me take the wheel."

He pressed his lips together, hating what he

was about to say because it just reinforced his feelings of guilt. If he hadn't done what he did next, his parents would still be alive and everything that had happened in the last twelve years—all the pain, all the hurt, all the estrangement—none of it would have ever happened.

Everything was *his* fault.

Dan's mouth felt like cotton and he could swear that his tongue felt like it was sticking to the roof of his mouth.

"What did you do?" Anne asked gently, prodding him to talk.

Dan took a deep breath, as if that would somehow shield him.

It didn't.

An almost surreal feeling came over him as he spoke. "I called my parents. I told them what was going on and where we were." He sighed, the guilt all but choking him. "I ratted my brothers out."

She wouldn't allow him to see it that way, to blame himself. "You *had* to tell your parents. From what you're telling me, neither one of them was in any condition to drive home. They could have killed themselves and you, or they could have killed somebody else."

She could see by the look in his eyes that

what she was saying wasn't helping him cope with the tragedy. But at least he was getting it all out.

"What happened next?" she urged.

Dan closed his eyes for a moment. Though he tried to distance himself from the event, he was reliving every moment of it.

"Dad sounded pretty angry when I told him what was going on. He told me not to let Luke and Bailey out of my sight. Then he said that he and Mom were coming to get us." He let out a long, shaky breath. The words all but stuck in his throat. "They never got there."

He looked up, expecting to see condemnation in Annie's eyes. But there was only sympathy.

She didn't understand, he realized. "Don't you see? If I hadn't called my parents, they would have never been on the road, never been in the wrong place at the wrong time. Never been hit by that drunk driver."

Dan looked away from her, so guilt-ridden he could hardly breathe. "I killed my parents," he told her in a hoarse whisper.

"No, you didn't," Anne insisted fiercely. "All you're guilty of was trying to look out for your brothers."

He'd been over and over this in his mind a hundred times in the last dozen years. "Maybe if I had looked out for my brothers and hadn't let them drink, or maybe if I never called my parents and instead made Luke and Bailey stay put until they were sober again and could drive home, my parents would still be alive. Or what if I hadn't gone out with my brothers? Then I wouldn't have known they were drinking and I wouldn't have had to call my parents to come get us."

"Then Luke and Bailey might have been killed trying to get home," Annie pointed out.

"Maybe not," he countered. "But my parents would have still been alive."

She felt his desperation. "Danny, you're going to drive yourself crazy with all these conjectures." Her eyes searched his face and saw how tortured he was. "You *have* driven yourself crazy with all these what-ifs. Don't you see? You've got to stop torturing yourself like this."

"But I'm the one responsible for their accident," he insisted.

"No, you are *not*. You didn't make that drunk driver plow into them. Maybe if someone had called *his* parents or someone else to come get him, then *he* wouldn't have been driving and he wouldn't have killed anyone. All you were ever guilty of was trying to think like a responsible person."

Anne moved closer to him on the sofa, wrapping her hand around his. "Oh, Danny, I wish you would have told me about this right from the beginning. I could have been there for you, supported you. We could have faced this terrible thing together. And then you could have saved yourself all this useless pain and anguish that you've been going through all these years."

And spared both of us more than a decade of loneliness, she added silently.

"I never told anyone," Dan said, his voice barely above a whisper. "Because then they'd know that it was my fault that my family was destroyed."

"You didn't destroy them," Anne stressed. She had to make him see that. "And there was more than one family at stake," she added quietly, thinking of Janie and the life the three of them could have had together.

Danny met her gaze and he saw that there were tears in her eyes. He assumed that she was referring to them and the family they could have created if he'd remained in Rust Creek Falls.

"I'm sorry, Annie. Sorry for everything. Sorry I left you," he whispered.

The compassion he saw in her eyes drew him in. Before he could summon all the reasons he shouldn't be doing this, he did.

He kissed her.

Because after a whole decade with nothing but memories to sustain him, there was nothing he wanted to do more at this very moment than to kiss her.

To show her how much he still cared about her.

He was afraid that if he did, she would pull away from him.

When she didn't, when she returned his kiss, he automatically deepened it. Framing her face with his hands, he was suddenly propelled back in time. Back to that last night they'd shared.

A myriad of urges and desires began to swirl through him like a twister picking up steam.

He'd missed her. Oh Lord, how he had missed her.

Missed this feeling.

Missed feeling alive.

He felt his blood surging through his veins, doing double time.

Old desires reared their heads, begging that he make up for lost time.

But as much as he wanted it, as much as he wanted *her*, he knew that he couldn't push, couldn't rush. Despite the temptation he felt through every inch of his body, this had to be entirely Annie's call and he would follow whatever signals she gave him.

Annie felt as if she was on fire.

Kissing Danny was even more wonderful than she remembered. It was as if she'd been sleeping all this time and, like the prince in *Sleeping Beauty*, he had woken her up, brought her out of her hibernation.

Every inch of her was tingling with desire. It was incredible that after all this time, she could vividly recall what it felt like to make love with him that one time. Every fiber of her being literally ached to do it again.

The thought sliced through her, frightening her so much that she found herself actually trembling. Not from desire, but from fear.

Summoning as much strength as she could, she pushed Dan away. "I can't!" she cried.

To his surprise, Dan realized that she was shaking. Annie *was* afraid of him. He'd never wanted that, never wanted her to be frightened of him. Did she actually think that he was going to force himself on her? Did she really believe that he had changed that much? That he would just grab what he wanted, ignoring decency?

"Annie, I never meant to—"

"Please leave." If she heard Dan out, she knew she'd succumb to him. To herself. And she couldn't afford to do that.

Dan wanted to talk to her, to explain that she had nothing to fear from him. To tell her what it meant to him to finally be able to open up to her the way he had.

But it was clear that somehow, he had managed to shake her up. Clear that somehow, signals had gotten crossed. Though he didn't understand *why* she felt this way, he definitely didn't mean for her to feel threatened by him.

He kept that to himself. Kept all his apologies to himself until he could find a way to deliver them without appearing threatening to her.

Murmuring, "I'm sorry," he let himself out the front door and left.

What the hell had just happened back there? he asked himself. He thought he had read all of Annie's signals correctly, but apparently he was no better at picking up signs now than he had been as a teenager. However, Annie was his best friend; she always had been. He didn't want to risk losing her now that he had finally gotten up the nerve to return to Rust Creek Falls and confront all his demons.

But maybe he already had lost her. Maybe Annie would be better off if he just went back to Colorado.

It looked like he had a great deal to think about, Danny told himself as he drove back to his brother's place.

Jamie. What was he going to tell his brother when Jamie asked how the evening had gone? Jamie had been the one who had insisted on having his best horses there for them so that Dan could take Annie for a ride the way he used to.

It was obvious that Jamie was determined to play Cupid for him. Too bad that right now, Cupid's arrows seemed to all be blunt-tipped.

What had she almost done? Annie thought, pulling her feet up under her on the sofa. If she hadn't pulled back when she had, she would have wound up making love with Danny—just like that.

Even after all this time, she would have made love with Danny in a heartbeat.

Hadn't she learned *anything*?

Even now, after he had gone, her heart was still pounding wildly.

She was afraid.

Very afraid. Because all it had taken was one kiss from Danny and she was ready to melt right there on the spot.

Anne blew out a breath, pulling herself together.

No matter how much she wanted to, she couldn't allow herself to lead with her heart. Not again. She absolutely refused to be that vulnerable a second time. Once had been more than enough.

Once had resulted in Janie coming into the world.

Janie.

Oh Lord, she still had to tell Dan about Janie. That he was Janie's father.

How was she going to do that without hurting Hank? And for all she knew, Danny might be angry with her for not telling him as soon as he had come back into her life. Never mind that she had tried as hard as she could to find him. Never mind that he was the one who had run out on her, not the other way around.

And there was Janie to think of. If she made this revelation, Annie's whole world could just come crashing down on her once she found out that her father wasn't Hank, but Dan.

So much to consider, she thought. And none of it clear.

Chapter 12

Keeping his distance from her was absolutely killing him.

He had promised himself after that last encounter between them that he would wait for Annie to make the next move no matter how long it took her.

Of course, if he was being honest with himself, Dan only expected that to take a day. Maybe two. But one day had come and gone, as had the second, and then the third, and still no resolution, no visit.

No Annie.

Maybe he'd been too optimistic about

all this. Maybe she wasn't going to make that "next move." Maybe Annie was actually grateful for this respite and intended to stretch it out as long as she could.

Possibly indefinitely.

Or maybe she was determined to wait him out until he finally decided to throw in the towel and went back to Colorado.

The more Dan thought about it, the more likely that last scenario seemed. He became afraid that it was over between them, really over.

Several times when he was at the tail end of his day, Dan had picked up the phone, thinking to call Annie and ask if he could come see her. He'd managed to talk himself out of it each time.

But the desire to see her was never far away. And it was getting progressively stronger.

After a week passed and still no call from Annie, Dan told himself that he had to face the inevitable: it was really over. He'd been a fool for thinking that they actually stood a chance of getting back together. And that, he knew, was on him, no one else.

He was still trying to decide whether it might be better for everyone all around if he just went back to Colorado early. The debate raged in his head one early morning as he prepared to meet Jamie out on the range. It felt like work on the ranch never seemed to be completed.

Leaving the house, he almost barreled right into Annie. Almost knocking her over, he quickly caught her in his arms, keeping her from hitting the ground. He was aware of his body fairly sizzling from the sudden, unexpected contact.

Let go of her! he silently ordered.

Still, it took him a moment to come around and release Annie. Clearing his throat, he said, "I'm sorry, I didn't know you were coming over."

He thought he heard her laugh softly. "That makes two of us," she confessed.

He wasn't sure he understood her meaning. All he knew was that, sudden or not, it was wonderful to hold her, even for a moment. Wonderful to see her.

Dan realized that there was silence between them. "I'm sorry, it's a little early in the morning for riddles." He stepped back, as if to check her over. "Are you all right? I didn't hurt you, did I?"

"You mean now? No." That had been a slip and she shouldn't have said that to him, she thought, upbraiding herself. "No," she repeated, adding, "you kept me from hitting the ground."

She was obviously here for a reason, he thought. Most likely to tell him something. Something he had a feeling he wasn't going to like hearing, based on the serious look on her face.

His survival instinct warned him that this wasn't going to be good. She was going to make it official, he thought. She was going to tell him not to come around anymore.

Damn, he should have left the house earlier.

Taking a breath, Annie plunged in, beginning slowly. "Danny—"

The least he could do was bail her out, he told himself. He wasn't going to let her suffer through this.

"Annie, you don't have to let me down easy," he told her. He saw her eyes widen. Probably because he'd guessed her reason for being here, he thought. "I know I was a fool for thinking I could just waltz back into town and pick up where we left off twelve years ago. I was a fool for thinking we still had a chance."

"I'm sorry, did I miss the part where you waltzed?" she asked.

He felt too tense, too sad, to laugh although he sensed she was doing her best to try to lighten the moment. But that really wasn't possible from his viewpoint.

"It's just an expression," he murmured.

"I know." Growing serious, Annie tried again. "We need to talk."

"And there's another expression," he noted sadly. "Probably one of the most dreaded expressions in the English language," he estimated. "But in this case, we don't really 'need to talk.' Don't worry, I won't be bothering you again."

Annie stared at him. Where was Danny getting this from?

"That's not what I came to say—and you're not bothering me," she added. "How could you be when I have been hoping for the last twelve years that you'd come back? What bothered me was that you left, not that you came back."

He was really confused now. "The other night, when I kissed you, you didn't act as if you were glad that I came back," he pointed out. "You acted as if you were afraid of me."

Annie shook her head. He was getting it all wrong. "No, I was afraid of being vulnerable."

Dan took that as an accusation. "I wouldn't have taken advantage of you," he told her. "You know me better than that."

"That's not what I mean by vulnerable."

Obviously he was tripping himself up. "Maybe I should just shut up and let you talk," he told her. "That way you can say what you've come to say."

Now that she had his full attention, fear undulated through her. Annie pressed her lips together, trying to gather her thoughts as well as her courage. It was one thing to tell herself she was going to tell Danny the truth—it was another thing entirely to actually find the words to do it.

Because once she said the words, she couldn't unsay them.

But Danny deserved to know. He had unburdened himself the other night and told her what had made him leave town and had kept him away for so long. The least she could do was tell him *her* secret. It was only fair.

"Can I help you get started?" he offered when he saw how much difficulty she was having beginning to impart whatever it was that she had come to say.

To his surprise, Annie laughed at his offer. It was a nervous laugh, but it was a laugh all the same.

"I think that's how the whole thing began," she told Danny, recalling that moonlit night when they had made love.

"No offense, Annie, but you're still not making any sense. *What* whole thing?" he wanted to know.

She took a deep breath. "Do you remember that last night we spent together?" she asked him.

Dan nodded. "The night before the accident." The night before his world turned to ashes.

"In more ways than one," Annie interjected, murmuring the words to herself.

Dan stared at her, utterly confused. "I don't understand. What are you telling me?"

"That night you made love to me?" she said, starting again. "Well, the evening had a slight by-product."

His eyebrows narrowed as he looked at her intently. All sorts of half-formed thoughts began running through his head.

"What kind of slight by-product?" he asked in a deadly quiet voice.

There was no way to say it but to say it, Anne told herself. She took a deep breath and let the words out. "You met her the first day you came over."

"Janie?" he asked in a disbelieving voice that was scarcely above a stunned whisper.

"Janie," Annie confirmed.

Danny stared at her, shell-shocked as he tried to understand the full import of what she was saying. "She's...?"

"Yours," Anne spelled out for good measure. "That night on the hilltop, my first time with you—with *anyone*," Anne stressed more for herself than for him, "we created a baby."

It felt as if his mind was stuck in first gear, unable to process, unable to go forward. "Janie's my daughter?"

"Yes."

His mouth had dropped open and it took effort to close it. He asked Anne the first question that flashed across his mind.

"Why didn't you tell me that I was a father?"

She almost laughed at that, but it really wasn't funny. He had no idea what she'd gone through when she'd realized that she was pregnant.

"I tried, Danny. Heaven knows, I tried. I asked everyone in town if they'd heard from you, including Bella and Jamie. But nobody had. It was as if you had fallen off the face of the earth right after the funeral."

"And Hank?" he asked Annie suddenly. "Does Hank know?"

"That Janie's yours? Yes, Hank knows," Anne told him, a sad smile curving the corners of her mouth. "But he married me anyway. He thought he could make me happy." But it hadn't worked out that way, she thought. Because she'd only ever loved one man. The man who stood before her.

Dan got up and began to pace around the room, too agitated to be able to remain seated.

Danny looked at her in disbelief. "My Lord, I'm a father," he said, dragging his hand through his hair as if that could help imbed the idea in his brain, make it take root. "I should have seen it. When I looked at her, I should have seen that she was mine."

She realized that he was blaming himself for the oversight. "People say she looks like me," Annie told him. "You said so yourself.

And don't forget, in your defense, you thought she was Hank's."

"And you didn't tell me any differently," he accused, cycling through disbelief, disappointment and anger. Trying to work his way through all those emotions to a safer, happier place because, after all, discovering that he had a child was supposed to be a happy event.

She knew that Danny didn't mean that the way it sounded. "That's not exactly a conversation opener, Danny. 'Hi, where have you been the last twelve years? And oh yes, by the way, you're a father.'"

He shook his head, his sanity coming back to him as his agitation began to ebb.

"You're right. Sorry. You're right," he repeated, doing his best to get a grip on himself. Brightening, he sounded almost eager as he asked, "What's she like?"

"You met her," she reminded him.

"Just for a second," he protested. Opinions couldn't be formed in a second. Neither could impressions. "Is she smart in school? Is she a handful? Does she have friends? Is she close to Hank?"

"One question at a time." Annie laughed, relieved to see that he was ultimately taking the news well. "Yes, yes, yes and—" She paused for a moment before saying, "Yes."

She knew Danny didn't want to hear the last answer, but she couldn't lie to him. Not after all this time. He deserved to hear the truth about everything concerning his daughter, even truths that weren't welcomed.

"I want to see her," Danny told her, excitement gathering in his voice.

He wanted to look at Janie as his daughter, not just Annie's.

"It's a school day. She's in class right now," Annie told him.

He wasn't thinking clearly. "Right. Okay, when she comes home," he amended. "I want to see her when she comes home."

She loved that he was happy about the news. But she hadn't told him everything and he had to hear it before they went any further. "I understand, but there's a problem, Danny."

He looked at Annie, his euphoria abruptly on hold. "I don't understand," he confessed. "What kind of a problem?"

This just wasn't getting any easier, Anne thought. She felt as if she was trying to slog her way through a five-foot-high snowdrift and she kept losing her footing.

"Janie doesn't know that you're her father," she said, watching his face carefully for any telltale signs of anger. "She thinks Hank is."

Dan had to admit it wasn't welcomed news, but it wasn't entirely unexpected, either. After all, when he'd met the girl, she hadn't given him any indication that she thought he was her father.

Nodding, he said, "I've got a lot of years to make up for."

"Yes, I know, but—"

He knew what Annie was going to say and he reassured her. "You're right, you're right. I've got to think about what's right for Janie. I want to tell her, but I don't want to turn her whole world upside down. She might even hate me for doing that and that's not what I want. I want to build a relationship with her. I want her to get to like me." He stopped abruptly and looked at Annie as it hit him again. "Wow, a daughter. I have a daughter." He became as eager as a kid at Christmas. "Do you have pictures of her? I mean when she was a baby and then a toddler?"

Annie smiled. She found his attitude rather sweet. "Yes, I have pictures."

"I want to see them," he told her. "Every one of them."

She laughed. This was, ultimately, what she had dreamed about, that he would welcome the news.

"That can be arranged. I have them in several albums. Would you like to see them now? I took the day off from work, thinking that maybe, if I told you about Janie and you didn't tell me to go to hell once you heard, that you might need to talk."

He looked at her, stunned by what she'd said in such an off-handed manner. "Why on earth would I tell you to go to hell?" he asked, totally puzzled.

Trying to be realistic, she'd played this scenario a hundred different ways in her head over the years. "Well, not everyone greets the idea of finding out they're a father in a positive light."

He knew that, but that wasn't him. The idea of having a family with Annie had once been a cherished dream of his. "I just really wish that there'd been a way for you to have let me know you were pregnant."

"So do I, Danny," she said, meaning that from the bottom of her heart. "So do I."

And then, rethinking the first time he saw Janie, he shook his head again. "I still don't see how I didn't see it the moment I saw Janie."

"Janie's small for her age. You probably thought she was younger than she is. Besides, there'd be no reason for you to suspect she's yours."

"When's Janie's birthday?" he wanted to know. When Annie told him, he grinned broadly. "She and I share the same month."

"Yes, I know." And then added, "And the same mouth."

That caught him off guard. He looked at Annie quizzically. "We do?"

"Uh-huh." She remembered looking at that small mouth for hours when Janie was a baby, wondering if she would grow up to look like Danny. "Look at it the next time you see her. Just don't stare," she cautioned.

"I won't stare," he promised. "But I do intend to see a great deal of her. I was serious about building a relationship with her."

Anne could feel her nervousness resurfacing. "Remember, we can't tell her you're her father until I think she's ready to hear that."

"Don't worry," he promised. "I won't tell her anything. I just want to get to know her and to get her to like me. That's just putting down groundwork, nothing more," he told her. "That's okay, isn't it?"

Annie nodded. "Yes, that's okay. I really appreciate you being patient about this."

He smiled. "I waited years to find out I was a father. I can wait a little longer to actually act like one."

Annie grew serious again. "I do have to warn you about something," she told him.

Dan told himself not to anticipate the worst. "What is it?"

"If she doesn't seem to respond to you, it's not you," she told him. "Janie's been a little down lately. Her best friend moved to France with her mother and her new dad recently and she can't seem to find a place for herself."

Dan appreciated the heads up. "Duly noted," he said. "My one immediate goal is to befriend her and to find a way to make sure she likes me. After that, we'll go from there. Deal?"

Anne smiled at him, more relieved than she could possibly say. "Deal."

Chapter 13

When she heard the knock on the door the first time, Janie just looked toward it with mild disinterest, expecting her mother to answer it even though she was in the kitchen, making dinner. As for her, she was busy watching one of her favorite programs, a show about a group of preteen girls who had superpowers.

But the second knock sounded more insistent. Muttering under her breath, Janie grudgingly paused the action on the TV and went to answer the door. Since her mother obviously hadn't heard the knock, answering the door was her superheroine good deed for the day.

Standing on her toes, she looked through the peephole to see who was on the other side. Reluctantly—because she knew her mother would want her to—Janie unlocked the door and pulled it open.

"Oh, it's you," she said by way of a bored greeting when she let Dan in. "Mom, your old boyfriend's here again," Janie shouted over her shoulder, then turned to face the less-than-welcome visitor again. "Mom's in the kitchen," she told him matter-of-factly. She pointed in the general direction as she closed the door, expecting him to go straight to the kitchen.

A thousand emotions were racing through Dan as he crossed the threshold, looking at Janie.

This was his daughter. His daughter. The thought almost paralyzed him. He made no move toward the kitchen.

After a beat, he found his tongue. "I didn't come to see your mother," he told her.

Janie was already walking away. Reaching the sofa, she took her seat again and hit the pause button on the remote control, unfreezing the action.

Following Janie, he walked into the living room behind her. His heart was pounding hard although he exercised extreme control over himself not to say or do anything to give himself away. "I came to see you," he told the girl even though she hadn't asked. He nodded at the TV. "What are you watching?"

"Ellie and Her Friends," she answered. And then she looked at him suspiciously. "Why?"

"I was just curious what you like to watch," he told her. It occurred to him that he had faced friendlier bucking broncos during his very brief rodeo days.

"No," Janie retorted impatiently, "why did you come to see me?" Her brilliant blue eyes were all but drilling holes into him.

"Because I'd like to get to know you," he answered. "I thought maybe we could be friends."

"So you can get my mom to like you again?" Janie demanded.

Janie was obviously not your typical eleven-year-old, he thought. No one was ever going to pull anything over on her. Which was a good thing, he thought, but not right at the moment.

"You think I'm underhanded?" he asked, then quickly explained, "That means sneaky."

Janie looked insulted. "I know what underhanded means. I'm not dumb."

Dan backtracked as quickly as he could, knowing that for better or for worse, today was going to be crucial in setting up the groundwork for a relationship between Janie and him.

"I'm sorry, I didn't mean to imply that you were," he told her.

"And," Janie continued with an imperious toss of her head, "I think all adults are sneaky. Except for my dad," she quickly amended. Her eyes bored into him, all but nailing him to the floor. "He thinks people should be honest with each other."

"Your dad's right," Dan agreed pleasantly. He knew this was a competition between Hank and himself, but he couldn't act like it. "People should be honest with each other. Is it all right if I sit down?" he asked, indicating the sofa.

Janie's small shoulders rose and fell in an indifferent shrug. "If you want to," she sniffed. She regarded him critically for a moment when he sat down on the sofa. "If you think people should be honest with each other, tell me the truth. Why do you want to get to know me?"

He knew this had to come out just right, otherwise the girl would go completely silent on him. "Because you're important to your mother and your mother is important to me."

A knowing, triumphant expression slipped over her small oval face. "You want her to be your girlfriend again."

"I want her to be my friend again," Dan deliberately corrected.

Baby steps, he told himself. *Baby steps*.

Janie looked as if she didn't believe him. "And if she says no, she doesn't want to be your 'friend,' you'll go away and forget all about me, so don't pretend you want to be *my* friend," she told him, annoyed.

"I'm not pretending," Dan insisted. "I do want to be your friend." *More than you could possibly guess*, he added silently.

Janie shifted on the sofa to look at him, her hands fisted at her waist. "Even if Mom won't be yours?"

"Even if your mom won't be mine," he assured his daughter.

"Huh!" Janie uttered the word as if it were

a grunt and said nothing for more than a minute as she went back to watching her program. Then, still keeping her eyes on the TV, she pointed to the dark-haired character who was currently talking. "That's Ellie," she told him. "She's the one who got her superpowers first. There was this magic meadow with this really strange silver rock…"

Dan tried not to grin. Instead, he solemnly listened as his daughter told him the origin of the group's superpowers, acting as if he was listening to her reveal the mystery of the Holy Grail. He hung on every one of her words because they were *her* words and she was imparting them to him.

As he listened, he couldn't get over the fact that he was listening to his daughter.

His daughter.

The very thought left him in complete awe. He felt as if he was seated beside an honest-to-goodness miracle. A miracle that had been created by Annie and him.

The very thought left him speechless—and incredibly grateful.

Janie abruptly stopped talking. She was staring at him. "You've got a funny look on your face," she told him. It was technically more of an accusation than a stated fact.

Dan quickly tried to explain away the look she was referring to. "I'm just really interested."

"Oh yeah?" It was obvious that she didn't believe him for a moment. "If that's true, then tell me what I just said. Tell me how the group all got their superpowers."

"Okay."

And then Dan proceeded to do just that, going back to the very first thing Janie had said and then continuing on to the very end. He left none of the five "superheroines" out. Finished, he smiled at his daughter.

The fact kept hitting him in waves. Just when he thought he was used to it, it hit again.

His daughter.

"Did I forget anything or leave something out?" he asked her, fairly certain that he hadn't.

The suspicion vacated those blue eyes of hers, replaced by wide-eyed wonder.

"No," she said, her voice tinged with disbelief. "No, you didn't. You were really listening."

"Sure. I told you I wanted to learn about the

program you were watching. I'd like to learn more if you'd like to tell me," he encouraged.

Dan was rewarded with a guileless smile. A smile that reminded him so much of Annie. It was clear that Janie was warming up to him, he thought happily, at least a little.

"Okay," she told him. "About Amanda—" And she was off and running.

Anne heard the entire exchange between Danny and Janie from the kitchen. It was really hard for her to stay out of the way like this. More than anything, she really wanted to go into the living room and watch her daughter interacting with Danny.

But she had given Danny her word that she would let him talk to Janie alone, at least this first time. To be honest, part of her had worried that Janie would clam up or sound off like a typical preteen even though she had raised the child to be respectful and polite.

After all, preteens were unpredictable.

She was happy to see that this was going far better than she had ever hoped.

Maybe Janie would learn to like Danny, she thought hopefully. If her daughter did, then maybe, just maybe, in time, they could tell her the truth: that Danny was her real father.

But not today. Definitely not today, Anne thought as she continued to prepare the chicken parmesan that was Janie's favorite dinner.

But someday, she thought, hugging the idea to her.

Maybe someday, if things went really, really well, they could finally get to be a real family, the way she'd dreamed so many times that they would be.

Anne finally ventured out of the kitchen an hour and a half later when she'd finished preparing dinner.

"Dinner's ready, Janie," she announced, stopping just short of the sofa.

Dan had progressed past Janie's favorite TV program and now he appeared to be in the middle of playing a video game with her. He was making moves like someone who had played video games all of his life. She knew for a fact that he hadn't.

Anne had to admit she was more than a little impressed by the display.

"You play video games?" she asked Dan.

"He almost beat me," Janie told her. To Anne's huge relief, there was no hostility in her daughter's voice. There was even a smattering of respect. "Not bad for a newbie."

Anne didn't bother trying to hide the smile that rose to her lips. "In case you don't know, she just gave you a huge compliment," she told Danny.

Dan inclined his head and smiled at the girl beside him. "Thank you."

"It's nothing," Janie told him carelessly.

"Well, you're having dinner so I'd better go," Dan said, retiring his game controller before rising to his feet. He nodded at his companion for the last hour and a half. "Janie, it's been a pleasure. Thanks for letting me spend the afternoon with you."

For a second, Anne thought that her daughter wasn't going to say anything in response. But then Janie spoke up in a nonchalant voice. "You can stay for dinner if you want." The girl's eyes shifted toward Anne. "That's okay, right, Mom?"

She wasn't going to cry, Anne told herself. She wasn't. But it wasn't easy.

Exercising extreme control over her emotions, Anne replied, "Yes, that's okay—if Mr. Stockton doesn't have any other plans for dinner."

Danny smiled broadly. "I can't think of a thing I'd rather do," he told Janie with a wink.

"But after dinner," Anne interjected, looking at her daughter as she repeated the familiar refrain, "you have to finish all your homework."

"I can do that after Danny leaves—I mean Mr. Stockton," Janie corrected herself when her mother gave her a reproving look.

"That's not how it works, Janie," Anne told her as all three of them went into the kitchen and she added a third place setting to the table. "You know how important it is for you to do your homework."

"Don't worry, I'll get it done," Janie insisted. "You know I'm smart."

"Maybe a little too smart for your own good," Anne countered.

Rather than argue with her mother, Janie turned her eyes toward her new friend.

Janie was looking for him to intercede, Dan realized. He didn't want to lose ground with the girl, but he didn't want to tread on territory that was clearly Annie's. After all, she was the one who had done all the heavy lifting, been there through everything from diapers to braces and everything in between.

"I don't really think there's such a thing as being too smart," he finally said, hoping that was diplomatic enough to appease both females. "But just to keep the peace, maybe you should do as your mom says. After all, she spent all that time making this really great meal for you."

Annie had told him that chicken parmesan was Janie's favorite so he felt he was on safe ground bringing the meal up to Janie.

Janie sighed, relenting. "Okay, I'll do my homework after dinner."

"That's my girl," Annie said fondly. She wanted to hug Janie, but she held herself in check, knowing Janie might be embarrassed if she was on the receiving end of any public displays of affection.

Janie rolled her eyes, "Yeah, yeah, let's eat!" she declared.

"Music to my ears," Dan said as he sat down at the table.

And mine, Anne thought, glancing first at her daughter, then at Danny.

Dan was being carefully optimistic, but there was no other way to view this.

His campaign to win his daughter over was going very, very well.

He'd been dropping by Annie and Janie's home in the afternoon for a week now and each time, he and Janie spent at least some time together.

In addition to playing the video games she loved and watching her favorite programs with her, Dan introduced his daughter to a few old-fashioned board games, ones he used to play when he had been Janie's age.

"These are ancient," Janie hooted when he had produced the first board game out of the backpack he had brought with him.

"I prefer to think of them as having withstood the test of time," he told Janie. He emptied out the backpack, taking out five board games in all. "It takes precision and skill to play these."

Janie looked at the boxed games disdainfully. "Not interested," she told him.

He was beginning to pick up subtle clues on how to deal with his daughter. "Not interested or afraid you're not good enough?" he challenged.

Janie tossed her head as she braced her shoulders. The girl was indeed her mother's daughter, Dan thought affectionately. Like Annie, Janie was unable to walk away from a challenge.

So they played the board games he brought and eventually they progressed to checkers, and then, finally, to chess.

When he first set up the board, Annie, who had taken to being around somewhere in the background for this interplay between Danny and their daughter, frowned. Intelligent or not, she thought that chess was far too difficult a game for someone Annie's age.

"Do you really think this is a good idea?" she asked Dan.

"Sure." A little taken aback by her protest, Dan continued to set up the pieces. "Why not?"

"Because it's *chess*," Annie stressed. "It requires a great deal of concentration. It's a game for adults, not eleven-year-olds."

Janie did not take her mother's intercession kindly.

"I'm not a baby, Mom," her daughter said, bristling at being dismissed so out of hand. "I can do it." Her eyes turned toward Dan, this time challenging *him*. "Teach me," she all but commanded.

A satisfied smile spread across his lips. "I fully intend to," Dan told the girl. Finished setting up the pieces, he put the empty box aside. "My dad taught me how to play when I was about your age," he told her. He'd really been twelve, but Annie didn't need to know that. "He loved the game but no one wanted to play with him, not even my mom. So he taught me how to play so he would always have someone to play against."

Danny expected her to ask why no one wanted to play his father. Instead, she had a different question to ask him.

"Were you good?" Janie wanted to know, scanning the way the pieces were laid out on the board.

Dan smiled nostalgically. "Good enough to beat him once or twice."

"Oh." By the expression on Janie's face it was obvious that wouldn't have been enough for her. "Too bad."

"No, that's good," he corrected Janie, "because my dad was a really top-notch player. Winning against him was really a big deal. The first time it happened, I was walking on air."

Even the skeptic, Janie suggested, "Maybe he let you win."

The girl was sharp, he thought. "I thought of that," he admitted. "But my dad said that letting me win wasn't teaching me anything. He always said that the wins you earn are the ones that really stay with you. Okay," he said, turning the board toward her, "are you ready to learn?"

He could swear her eyes were sparkling as she said, "Ready!"

"Then here we go," he said as he began to teach his daughter the basic moves of the game, just the way his father had taught him.

Chapter 14

"Just what were you thinking?" Hank demanded gruffly.

Annie bristled at his question. At least he'd waited until Janie had gone to her room to unpack from her sleepover at his ranch before he confronted her.

Startled by Hank's rare angry tone, the first thing Anne thought of was that her daughter had told him about Danny's frequent visits. She wasn't sure just how to answer him. Especially if, just in case, Hank was asking her about something else.

Glancing toward the rear of the house to

make sure Janie wasn't within hearing range, Anne told him, "I don't know what you—"

"Let me make this easy for you," Hank said angrily. "Janie told me that Daniel's been coming over pretty regularly these days. She says he's been teaching her how to play board games, like chess—"

Anne seized on the last part, trying her best to make Hank see how beneficial these visits were to Janie. "Chess is a very mind-broadening game."

Hank scowled, clearly not in the mood to be played for a fool. "Don't give me that, Anne. This isn't about chess and you know it. It's about him trying to wiggle his way into Janie's life."

"He just wants to get to know her, Hank." She lowered her voice even more, afraid that the sound of raised voices would bring Janie out of her room before she could get Hank to drop the subject. There was too much at stake here. "He's her father—"

"No," Hank retorted forcefully. "*I* am Janie's father."

"Nobody's disputing your place in her life, Hank," Anne stressed, still trying to calm him down. "She loves you. But he's missed so much—"

Hank made a dismissive, disparaging noise. "And whose fault was that?" he demanded. "He wasn't here, remember?" He grabbed hold of Anne's arms, as if doing so would somehow make her see reason. "Tell me, how do we know, after Janie gets all caught up in whatever tales he's spinning to win her over, that he won't just get it into his head to take off again? Have you thought about what that'll do to her?" Hank asked. "I don't want to risk this guy upsetting Janie for no reason." He looked into Anne's eyes. "I can't tell you what to do, Anne. But for the sake of our daughter—*our* daughter," he deliberately stressed, "I want you to think very hard about this."

He let her go and strode toward the door. But before he left, he looked at Anne sharply as he repeated, "*Very* hard."

Anne remained where she was standing long after Hank had closed the front door behind him. His words continued to echo in her head.

She hadn't wanted to admit it while Hank had berated the situation, pointing out what he felt was the obvious, but she was actually harboring the same fears that Hank had raised. And not just concerning Janie's reaction to Danny's possible disappearance from her life.

What if she were to get together with Danny, gave her heart to him the way she had before, and then he suddenly disappeared on her again the way he had twelve years ago? She had barely survived that at the time, but she had had a baby to think of and to take care of.

It was different this time. And she really didn't think her heart would be able to take that sort of abandonment a second time.

C'mon, Anne, he's not going anywhere. Look at how hard he's working to get Janie to like him, to build a relationship with her. That's not a man who's going to take off in the middle of the night. That's a man who's here to stay.

It made sense.

And yet…

"C'mon, it'll be fun," Anne coaxed, holding up a pirate costume that was clearly intended for a man to wear.

Dan looked at the costume dubiously. Along with the ruffled shirt and wide black pantaloons, Annie had a black eye patch attached to the hanger. "I don't know about this."

"The veterinary office is sponsoring a Halloween costume parade—emphasis on the word *costume*," Annie told him as well as her daughter. "That means you can't be in it unless you've got on some kind of a costume."

He saw the excitement on Janie's face, but he was still very reluctant to put on something that, in his judgment, made him look like a fool.

"I can stand on the sidelines and watch the parade," Dan offered, adding, "I'm really good at cheering and clapping."

"I'm going to be in it," Janie told him proudly. "I'm going as Ellie," she added, referring to the superheroine she'd told him about the first afternoon he had been over to her house.

"And I'll be your cheering section," Dan said, still hoping that was good enough. "Everyone needs a cheering section, even a superheroine."

He was weakening, Anne thought. She

could see it in his face. He really wanted Janie's approval.

"There'll be lots of people in town who'll be on the sidelines," she told Danny, then emphasized, "This is your time to step up for Janie."

"Where are you going to be?" Dan wanted to know. And then it hit him why she was so adamant about having him dress up. "Wait, don't tell me, let me guess. *You're* going to be on the sidelines, watching us."

"Hardly," Anne countered. "I have to organize and dress up some of the tamer pets whose owners want them to be in the parade." She paused, then added what she felt was the proper inducement. "Dr. Smith's bulldog is going to be wearing army fatigues."

Dan laughed as he tried to picture that in his mind. He'd seen the animal, a large, squat dog whose expression reminded him of one of the guests at the dude ranch this summer, a disgruntled man who'd found fault with everything during his entire vacation. "I guess that'll be worth the price of admission."

"They're charging admission?" Janie asked, puzzled as she looked at her mother.

"It's an expression, honey. Danny is being funny—or trying to be," Anne told her.

In the last few days, she had relented and allowed her daughter to refer to Danny by his first name. She'd decided the familiarity might make the ultimate transition from family friend to father a little easier in the long run.

At least she could hope that it would.

"I guess that is kind of funny," Janie agreed, glancing in his direction.

"I knew that seeing the bulldog in fatigues would change your mind," Anne told him.

"It didn't change my mind," Danny contradicted. He looked toward Janie before he said, "Actually, the opportunity to walk beside 'Ellie' in the parade was what changed my mind. I've always had a weakness for superheroines," he said, winking at Janie.

Janie giggled, obviously pleased.

It was a sound that she rarely heard of late coming from her daughter, Anne thought. Hearing it now really heartened her.

Maybe this *was* going to turn out well after all, Anne thought, despite all of her fears.

"We could all really use this diversion," Anne told her daughter and Danny. "It's been an utter madhouse at the lately clinic. I don't *ever* remember it being this busy."

"Why don't you just hire more vets to help you?" Janie asked.

"Out of the mouths of babes," Danny commented with a grin. He saw the indignant look that crossed Janie's face and could guess at what she was thinking. "Just another expression," he quickly said so she wouldn't think he was insulting her. "There's no way that I'm saying you're a baby. No one who can play chess the way you can could possibly be mistaken for a baby."

And he meant what he said. Janie had been getting really good at the game, absorbing everything he taught her like the proverbial sponge. He was in fact rather in awe of the girl's ability to think several moves ahead the way she did, given her age.

Janie looked properly placated. "Okay," she said, graciously accepting his explanation. Turning toward her mother, she asked, "So, are you going to be getting more vets?"

Anne nodded. "Dr. Smith is definitely trying to. He just asked Dr. Hadley Strickland, a friend of his who practices in Bozeman, to fill in at the clinic while she's here visiting over the Thanksgiving holiday," she told them. "He's hoping that might wind up convincing her to stay on."

"But that's just one person," Janie wisely protested. "You need more than one person, right, Mom?"

Dan decided to help Annie out.

"Right," he answered, joining in. "But it's a start," he pointed out. "Maybe if they can get this Dr. Strickland to come work at the clinic, she might know of someone else who Dr. Smith can hire, as well."

Anne said wistfully, "While he's at it, I hope Dr. Smith can see his way clear to hiring an assistant for the reception desk."

"Are you quitting, Mom?" Janie asked in what could only be taken as alarm. The girl had never reacted well to change and having her mother quit her job at the clinic was definitely a major change.

"Oh no, I love my job. How could I leave a bulldog in fatigues?" Anne teased. "But it would be nice to have a little extra help when it gets crazy at the clinic." She slipped her arm around her daughter's shoulders. "I like coming home with some energy to spare for my girl while she still wants to hang around with her old mom."

"You're not old, Mom," Janie said, speaking up quickly. And then she qualified with a mischievous grin, "Not exactly."

"I'll show you who's old," Anne declared. Grabbing her daughter, she pulled the girl closer to her and tickled her.

She let Janie go after a minute, knowing that the girl wanted to retain some of her new "dignity" around Danny.

"In Janie's defense, you did start it by referring to yourself as 'old,'" Danny pointed out.

That earned him a wide smile from Janie.

"Two against one, no fair," Anne cried. And then she suddenly remembered to look at her watch. It was getting late. "C'mon, you two, you have to get into your costumes," she urged. "You don't want to be late for the parade."

Danny gave her a look. "Try me."

"I bet I can get into my costume faster than you can," Janie declared, cheerfully challenging him.

With a resigned sigh, Dan took the pirate costume from Anne, who was holding it out toward him. He made no effort to hide the disdainful look on his face. "Who came up with this whole costume idea anyway?"

"Dr. Smith," Anne reminded him as she went to get her own costume that she'd left hanging in her room.

"No, I mean originally," Dan said, calling after her, "way back in time."

"Probably some very bored people," Anne guessed just before she closed her bedroom door. She regarded her costume for a moment, hoping it would knock Danny's boots off.

He supposed it was worth it, Dan thought as he finished putting on his costume. Wearing this would make his daughter happy, and after all that *was* his ultimate goal—making Janie happy and getting her to accept him into her life. He knew it was still a big leap from there to telling her that he was her father, but he needed all the goodwill he could build up.

And if looking like an idiot, he thought, regarding his reflection in the mirror, helped contribute to that goodwill, so be it.

Damn but he hated Halloween, Dan thought as he walked out of the bathroom. He was carrying his own clothes folded up under his arm.

He encountered Janie first. She was standing in the living room, wearing her blue costume and flowing cape, her hands fisted on her waist. She looked like the very picture of confidence.

Dan pretended to do a double take when he saw her. "Wow, Ellie, have you seen Janie around anywhere? I know that she'd love to get your autograph," he told the girl, doing his best to maintain a straight face.

Her eyes sparkled as she giggled. "Danny, it's me, Janie."

Dan pretended to look around the room as if he were trying to locate the source of the voice.

"Janie? Are you here somewhere?" he said, pretending to be mystified. "I hear your voice, but I don't see you."

Janie tugged on his sleeve. "Right here, silly. It's me. *I'm* Janie. This is just my costume."

"Wow, it looks so realistic," he cried. "I really thought that you were Ellie."

"No, you didn't," Janie told him. But she was fairly beaming over his reaction to her costume.

"Where's your mom?" Dan asked. "She's

the one who was trying to get us to hustle and it looks like she's the one who's still getting dressed."

He saw Janie grinning just before he heard the voice coming from behind him.

"No, I'm not. I'm right here. Behind you."

Dan turned around, expecting to see Annie wearing something mundane, like scrubs, which would have been the easiest costume for her. Or maybe some furry costume so she could look like one of the animals that were treated regularly by the vets at the clinic.

He was *not* prepared for the pirate hat with its jaunty feather, the tall black high-heeled boots or the short, willowy skirt topped with a laced-up black velvet vest over a white blouse with wide, flowing sleeves.

"Are you a pirate, too, Mom?" Janie asked.

"Actually, I'm a pirate *queen*. I thought of being a superheroine," she said matter-of-factly, "but I didn't want to steal your thunder. This is better," she told her daughter.

"A lot better," Dan commented, his eyes sweeping over her appreciatively.

All he had seen Annie wearing up until now was her vet clinic uniform, or a pair of jeans with a baggy sweater draped over them.

He'd forgotten just how sexy she had looked back when they were going together in high school.

As a matter of fact, she looked even better now than she had back then. So much so that he was having trouble taking his eyes off her.

"Does that make me a pirate king?" he asked her.

"No, you're just a regular pirate," she told him. "That means I get to order you around."

He leveled a questioning look at her. "And this is different how?"

Janie giggled again.

Anne pointed toward the door. "C'mon, you two, let's go. Like I said, we don't want to be late."

"Yes, we do," Danny said as he followed them out the door. In fact, he'd rather not go at all. He would much rather spend the time right here, getting reacquainted with the pirate queen.

But there was Janie to think of, so, with a muted, resigned sigh, he closed the front door behind him and then followed Annie and their daughter to the car.

Chapter 15

A whole myriad of emotions were vying for top position within Anne when they arrived home, none of them good. There was sadness, disappointment and a feeling of rejection. And all the emotions were centered around her daughter.

It hadn't started out that way.

Janie, Danny and she had had an incredibly wonderful afternoon, joining in the costume parade that had been sponsored by the vet clinic. Afterward they returned to the clinic, where they'd handed out candy to the excited trick-or-treaters who'd come by the downtown businesses.

Since this was Halloween, the day's festivities were to culminate with her taking Janie out trick-or-treating to several of the neighbors' homes the way they had done ever since her daughter was three and had first begged to take part in the sugar-laden holiday.

At least, Anne had assumed that the day would end this way.

But Janie apparently had different ideas.

"Please, Mom," Janie begged. "Why can't I go trick-or-treating with my friends? All the other kids in my class are breaking up into groups and doing it."

Anne hated saying no to Janie, but she was concerned for her daughter's safety. She was also reluctant to give up a much-loved tradition.

"I'm sorry, Janie. But you're just too young to go out after dark with only a few girls with you," Anne said firmly.

Janie was quick to tell her, "Cassie's mother is coming with us."

"Cassie's mother," Anne repeated. She had been replaced by another girl's mother, she thought. That really stung and though she tried not to, she took it personally.

Dan had stayed silent, trying his best to keep out of the exchange between mother and daughter. He heard what was being said and heard, too, what *wasn't* being said. He could hear that Annie was clearly hurt because Janie wanted to go trick-or-treating with another mother acting as a chaperone, not her.

Still, he could see Janie's point. She'd spent the afternoon with her mother and although it had been a lot of fun—she'd clearly looked as if she was having a good time—now she wanted to spend some time with her friends. It was all a part of growing up.

Though he felt for both sides, he still would have gladly remained on the sidelines, letting this play out without his input.

But then Janie completely surprised him by turning to him and asking him to back her up.

"Tell her to let me go, Danny," she pleaded. "I'll only be gone for a couple of hours."

"A couple of hours?" Anne echoed.

There weren't that many doorbells to ring in the neighborhood. What was her daughter going to be doing with her friends that would last for a couple of hours?

Danny decided to pick a side—kind of.

"You know how it is," he said to Annie. "Kids just want to enjoy themselves."

Anne looked at her daughter. She wanted to put her foot down and veto this, but having Janie angry and upset with her wasn't the way she wanted to end the evening, either.

"How many girls are going?" she finally asked her daughter.

"Eight," Janie said, then promptly named every one of them.

Listening to her, Annie frowned. "I don't know if Cassie's mother is up to handling eight girls on her own."

"Oh, she's up to it," Janie assured her with enthusiasm. "And Cassie's mom is strict," she added, using that as a winning argument. "The only way Cassie could go trick-or-treating with the rest of us was if her mother came along to make sure we behaved."

"I like this woman's style already," Anne commented, although she wished that *she* was the chaperone, not Cassie's mother. Seeing how much this meant to Janie, she sighed. "Okay, you can go—as long as you promise to behave yourself. And if anything goes wrong, anything at all," she emphasized,

"I want you to call me immediately, understood?"

Janie looked at her, all eleven-year-old innocence wrapped in fledgling eagerness. "What could go wrong, Mom?"

"You never know," Anne informed her. "Do I have your word?"

Janie rolled her eyes. "Yes, I'll call you if anything goes wrong—but it won't," she added insistently.

"All right," Anne reluctantly agreed. "I'll drop you off at Cassie's house."

"No, you don't have to," Janie protested. "Her mother's coming here to pick me up. She's picking up all the girls."

"See?" Danny said, doing his best to nudge her into coming around. "What could be better?"

What could be better is if I was the one taking the girls, not this other woman.

Anne gave him a less-than-happy look, but said nothing.

Just then, the doorbell rang and Janie scrambled to grab the slightly worn plastic pumpkin she used every year to collect her treats.

"That's Cassie's mom now!" she declared,

holding onto the pumpkin and rushing toward the door.

"You wait for me," Anne ordered, quickly following in Janie's wake.

But Janie had already thrown open the front door, clearly eager to make her escape.

"Hi," she said brightly, greeting the woman in the doorway. "Mom said I could go!"

Cassie Jackson's mother, a rather big-boned woman with a quick smile, was dressed as Cinderella's fairy godmother.

"Don't worry about a thing. I'll watch each and every one of them as if they were my own," the woman promised, putting an arm around Janie and shepherding the girl out the door.

"Bye," Anne called after her daughter. "Be sure to listen to Mrs. Jackson and have fun."

But Janie didn't seem to hear her. She was already getting into Mrs. Jackson's station wagon, chattering happily with her friends.

Anne sighed as she closed the door.

"And so it begins," she murmured, saying the words more to herself than to Dan.

"So what begins?" he asked her, not sure he understood what she was saying.

Anne turned from the door. "Janie growing up, becoming independent. Once it starts, there's no stopping it," she said sadly.

"She's eleven," Dan reminded her gently. "She's just going trick-or-treating with her friends, she's not going away to college."

"Yet," Anne qualified sadly. "But it'll happen faster than you think." Crossing back to the living room, she sank down on the sofa, the very picture of resigned sadness. "And much faster than I'm ready for," she added quietly.

Dan sat down beside her. She looked so unhappy, it tore at his heart. He slipped his arm around her shoulders, attempting to offer Annie at least a little comfort.

"It's a long way between trick-or-treating and college, Annie. You'll have time to adjust," he promised her.

Annie said nothing. She just mutely nodded her head. He looked down at her and saw the light glistening on her cheek.

"Are you crying?" he asked, surprised.

Averting her face, she shook her head and managed to get out a small "No" in response.

"Yes, you are," he contradicted. Crooking his index finger beneath her chin, he raised her head and turned it toward him. "You're crying."

Annie jerked her head away. "So what?" she retorted angrily.

"Oh, Annie," he said compassionately, "you can't keep her little forever."

"I didn't want forever," she protested. "I just want a little longer, that's all." She was doing her best to stop the flow of tears. But they insisted on coming.

Danny took her into his arms then and held her closer. She attempted to pull away, then just gave up and sagged against him.

"I know," he said understandingly. "But at least you had more years than I had. You got to see all the things that I missed seeing. You got to make memories," he told her.

Her head on his shoulder, she turned to him then, too overcome with emotion to say a word.

Desperately wanting to comfort her, to somehow absorb her pain, Dan found himself lowering his mouth to hers.

And just like that, the years melted away and they were eighteen again. Eighteen without the restraint of any of the shackles that life had forged for them along the way.

The kiss, beginning slowly and deepening, seemed to unlock all the desire he had kept so carefully locked away. The desire that had been branded with her name on it all these years.

Adrenaline surged through his veins, fueling the passion that was growing and multiplying in every fiber of his being.

He wanted to trace her curves, the contours of her body with his lips. He wanted to make up for all the time that they had lost.

Every kiss just intensified his desire for her, stirring it up to a fever pitch.

He wanted to make love to her as if there was no tomorrow, no consequences to face. Nothing but the raw need and passion that was even now pounding through his veins in sheer anticipation of her and what lay ahead.

As he felt her hands against his chest, it was all he could do not to strip that blood-stirring costume she was wearing from her body.

But it was exactly those hands pressed against his chest that suddenly had him screeching to a halt emotionally and pulling back.

Breathing heavily, her lips all but throbbing from the imprint of his, Anne looked up at him in complete confusion and bewilderment.

"What's wrong?" she cried. "Why did you stop?"

"I can't do this," Danny told her. "I can't force myself on you like this."

The hurt look on her face faded as she realized that he wasn't rejecting her. Ever noble, he was protecting her.

"You're not forcing yourself on me," she told Danny, her breath all but coming in snatches. "I've been waiting for this—for you—for twelve years."

Annie took hold of the front of his shirt and pulled him closer to him. His kiss had instantly triggered the hunger she had struggled to suppress since she had first seen him standing on her doorstep, back in town after all these years.

She had been eagerly anticipating this since that moment.

Yes, she was afraid—with good reason, she felt—but at the same time, now that Danny had rekindled the fire she had been trying so hard to put out, she felt as if she was going to totally self-destruct if he did the noble thing and walked away from her.

She couldn't bear it.

Her eyes held his as she asked, "Are you going to make me beg?"

"No, never that," he told her.

Danny knew that his conscience was still going to bother him. But there was no denying that he wanted Annie so badly, he physically ached. He knew he would have absolutely no peace if he didn't give in to this incredible craving that threatened to consume him.

Surrendering, Dan began to make love to her then, softly, gently, reining in the all but insatiable desire to take her quickly, with wild abandonment.

He wanted to make sure that she would have no regrets, no doubts, even for a moment, over what was happening here between them. He didn't want to risk her believing that he was doing this just to satisfy himself, thinking that his first and foremost thought was not of her.

Because it was.

He had always placed her happiness, her fulfillment above his own, and having Annie achieve that fulfillment would make him happy and contribute to his own feeling of satisfaction.

Danny kissed her over and over again, feasting on her lips, on her throat, on the swell of her breasts as he slowly removed each piece of her pirate costume until all of it finally lay on the floor beside the sofa.

He ran his hands lovingly over her body, stroking it as if he were reverently stroking the strings of a priceless instrument, desperate to coax a beautiful melody out of it.

Annie twisted and turned beneath his hands. She loved the way he touched her, loved how he was making her body veritably hum with anticipation.

Unable to restrain herself any longer, she undressed Danny, curbing her eagerness in order not to tear anything. Her eagerness almost got the better of her not once but several times.

The less clothing there was between them, the greater her desire mounted until she felt as if she were on the verge of erupting. Like a wild woman, she raised her body, pressing up against his, silently urging him to take her.

And still he went slowly, even though she felt his urgent desire pressed against her body.

Over and over again, she sealed her mouth to his, her fingertips digging into his shoulders as she silently offered herself to him.

Dan resisted for as long as he could, wanting to prolong this moment for both of them. Once this lyrical dance was over and the passion spent, who knew the next time they would come together as one.

But he could only hold back for so long. And when Annie opened for him, her silent invitation clear, the last of his restraint shredded.

He entered her, his mouth sealed to hers just as his soul had been sealed to hers all these years.

He began slowly but the rhythm sped quickly with each moment, each thrust, until they were racing breathlessly toward the culmination of this union.

Racing toward the top of the mountain and to journey's end.

As the goal was finally reached, as stars exploded and rained down all around them, they held tightly onto one another. Euphoria wrapped itself around them, curtaining them in a private world of sensation and ecstasy.

They held reality at bay for as long as they could. Each was willing to freeze time at this very second while life-affirming sensations made their blood rush and their heads whirl.

Dan held Annie to him so tightly he could

literally feel her heart pounding against his. In that moment all he could think of was that he should have returned to Rust Creek Falls a lot sooner.

Because Annie—and this—was all that made life worth living.

He felt her sighing against him and knew that she was coming back down to earth, same as him. Even so, he wanted to hold her a little longer, pretend a little longer that this was how it was supposed to be—and had been since the beginning.

When she stirred, all he could think of was that he wanted to do it again, wanted to make love with Annie again.

And again.

And again after that, until he expired in her arms. Because right now, he couldn't think of a better way to go than in Annie's arms, making love with her.

Chapter 16

"We've got to get dressed," Annie cried, suddenly bolting upright and hitting the top of her head against Danny's chin.

Jolted, he shook his head, trying to get his bearings.

Rubbing his chin, he said, "Not exactly the reaction I was hoping for." He'd been kissing her, arousing himself as well as, he'd hoped, Annie.

Annie had already scooped up her clothes from the floor, trying not to panic.

"Why aren't you moving?" she demanded. "Janie could be back any minute," she said, hurrying back into her pirate queen costume. She pushed his costume toward him urgently. "This is *not* the way I want to introduce her to her father."

He stopped dead, surprised. "Then you *do* want to tell her that I'm her father?" Annie had made it sound as if that revelation was a long way off.

She pulled on her vest. "Yes, of course," she answered.

The prospect of being able to finally tell Janie that he was her father excited him. "When?" Danny wanted to know.

Anne's eyes met his. After the last hour they had just spent together, she didn't think she had to draw him a picture.

"I think that's pretty clear," she told him. When Danny continued looking at her, obviously waiting for an answer as he pulled his boots on, she said, "Now."

He didn't want her to feel pressured. "Are you sure about this?" he asked her.

"Very sure," she told him. And then it occurred to her that *he* might not want to tell Janie yet. "Why, are you having second thoughts about this?"

"Me?" he asked, surprised. "No. I just don't

want you to rush into anything you're possibly going to wind up regretting, that's all. I don't want to lose all the ground I've gained with you—and with Janie."

"That's just it," she said as she finished dressing and started straightening up the sofa. "She likes you. Sometimes I think Janie likes you better than she likes me." She smiled at him as she arranged the throw pillows. "And you and I seem to have mended our fences. I don't see any reason to keep this from her any longer. Janie deserves to know the truth," she concluded.

"Well, you won't get any argument from me," Danny told her.

"Good." She raised her head, alert as she listened intently. "Because I think I hear a car pulling up."

Annie's heart was in her throat as she went to the front door and opened it. She was just in time to see Janie coming up the front walk.

The girl paused to wave goodbye to Mrs. Jackson and whatever girls were still in the van. And then, as the van pulled away, Janie ran up to her mother, her face flush with excitement, the plastic pumpkin she'd taken with her utterly stuffed with candy.

"Did you have a good time?" Annie asked her daughter, ushering her in.

"The best!" Janie answered. "I got a ton of candy!" She held up the pumpkin as proof, then she walked into the house ahead of her mother. "Look!" she said to Danny, showing him the pumpkin.

"Looks like a ton all right," he agreed.

"Which you will ration out over the next week or so," Annie instructed.

Two years ago, Janie had gotten sick to her stomach, gorging herself on sweets, and Anne didn't want a repeat of that event, especially not tonight.

Janie sighed. "Yes, Mother, I know the drill." She offered contents of the pumpkin to Danny. "Want some?" she asked.

It was all Dan could do not to hug his daughter. There would be time enough for that later, he promised himself.

"You first," he told her.

Janie grinned. "Okay." Taking a large candy bar near the top of the heap, she then held the pumpkin out to Danny again. When he took a small piece, she turned toward her mother. "Mom, you want some candy?"

"Maybe later, honey." Her stomach was far

too tied up right now. "Janie, I need you to sit down," she told her daughter. "Over here, on the sofa." She patted the seat beside her. Once they were all sitting down, Anne said, "We need to talk."

Janie stopped picking through her newly acquired stash and looked up at her mother. Wariness entered her blue eyes.

"Why?" she asked nervously. "What's wrong?"

"Nothing's wrong. I just— We just," Annie corrected herself, glancing over her daughter's head at Danny, "think it's time that you knew something."

Janie put the overflowing pumpkin on the coffee table and looked from her mother to Danny and then back to her mother.

"You're getting married, aren't you?" she guessed, catching both adults off guard. Janie shrugged carelessly. "I knew there was a reason Danny was here so much." She shrugged again, trying very hard to be blasé. "I guess it's okay."

Annie came very close to losing her nerve. After all, Janie had just given her a way out. It would be easy to accept her daughter's take on this and just let it go for now.

But she knew she couldn't put this off indefinitely, not after getting involved with Danny again, after finding out that the intensity of her feelings for him hadn't lessened. No, she needed to tell her daughter the truth right now.

"That's not the reason that he's been here so much." She raised her eyes to Danny, silently asking him to step in and say something to back up what she was trying to tell Janie.

"I wanted to get to know you, Janie," he told his daughter.

Janie clearly looked confused. "I don't understand. If it's not because you want to marry my mom, then why would you want to get to know me?"

They were back to the same question she had asked the first time he had come over to see her.

Anne drew in a breath and plunged in. "Because he's your father."

Instantly, Janie's expression became a mask of disbelief and anger.

"No, he's not! Hank's my father!" she insisted vehemently. "My father comes to pick me up for sleepovers every week," she cried, as if that was all the proof she needed.

"Hank's your stepfather, honey," Anne told her. She tried to put her hand on Janie's shoulder, but the girl jerked away, furious.

Janie's eyes were blazing as she cried, "Why didn't you tell me?"

"Well, at first there was no reason to," Anne said. "And then, even after the divorce, Hank was so crazy about you, I saw no reason to tell you. But now that your father has come back to Rust Creek Falls—"

"You lied to me!" Janie shouted at her, jumping to her feet. Her fury took in both adults. "You both lied to me!"

"We didn't lie to you, Janie. We just didn't know how to tell you. We were afraid of upsetting you," Danny told her, trying to reason with the girl.

"Well, guess what? I'm upset!" Janie spat out. "I hate you! I hate you both!" she shouted angrily. "And I'm calling Dad and telling him to come get me. I'm going to go live with him!"

Before Anne could stop her, Janie dashed out of the room and ran to her bedroom. She slammed the door. The sound reverberated throughout the house.

Stricken, Anne looked in the direction

that her daughter had taken. "Well, that went well," she said, her voice breaking on the last word.

"I'll go talk to her," Danny offered, beginning to head toward Janie's room.

Annie caught his arm, holding him back. "No, don't. It's not going to do any good now," she told him in a hollow voice. She blew out a ragged breath, all but collapsing onto the sofa. "I knew it was going to go like this. That's why I put off telling Janie all this time." There were tears in her eyes as she looked at Danny. "But this is even worse than I imagined. She's going to move in with Hank." She felt as if each word she uttered was cutting up her insides.

"Oh, Annie, I'm so sorry." Danny attempted to take her in his arms, but she shrugged out of his hold, pulling away. He dropped his hands to his sides. "We'd been getting along so well, I really hoped that when she finally knew I was her father, she'd accept it even if she didn't welcome it right away. Please believe me, I never meant to hurt anyone. I just thought… I thought if I came back…"

He was unable to finish, because he felt

that no matter what his intentions had been, it didn't matter. What mattered was that Annie was crushed and their daughter wanted nothing to do with either of them. And it was all his fault.

"I should have just stayed away," Danny said, guilt all but suffocating him because of this latest turn of events.

He looked down at Anne huddled on the sofa in a fetal position. Her heart was clearly broken because her daughter wanted to go live with the man she regarded as her father. He knew Annie well enough to know that she wouldn't stop the girl, wouldn't force Janie to stay with her.

If he hadn't come back, none of this would have happened.

He wanted to apologize again. Wanted to tell her that he would have rather died than caused her this pain.

But nothing he said would change anything. The best thing he could do right now was leave.

Opening the door, he let himself out. Annie was still on the sofa, in shock and staring at the rear of the house as he closed the door behind him.

* * *

Hank came to pick Janie up less than an hour later. Janie flew into his arms and held on tightly. "I want to live with you, Dad."

He hugged the girl to him, looking accusingly at Anne over her daughter's head.

He had arrived here so quickly, Anne had no doubt that Janie had filled him in on everything.

She didn't have long to wait before finding out.

"Take your suitcase and wait for me in the truck, Janie," Hank told the girl.

"Sure, Dad," she answered.

Janie left without so much as a backward glance or a single word to her mother.

Anne stared after her, feeling as if her heart had been slashed open with a jagged knife.

"I warned you," Hank said the moment Janie closed the front door behind her. "I told you that no good would come of telling Janie the truth. She didn't need to know that Daniel is her birth father."

"I didn't like lying to her," Anne told him, doing her best not to fall apart.

"You weren't lying to her," he retorted. "You were shielding her from a harsh reality that she was far too young to know. Or to understand."

"And how old should she have been before she found out?" Anne wanted to know, getting defensive.

Except for the last incident—also centered around Dan—she rarely saw Hank get angry, but he was angry now. An angry Papa Bear protecting his cub with unsheathed claws.

This was about the little girl he loved dearly and Hank intended to keep her safe, emotionally and physically, at all cost.

"With luck, never," Hank answered. "There was no reason for her to know who Daniel was. She was a happy, well-adjusted little girl who had two parents who loved her."

"Now she has three," Annie answered defiantly.

"And she's not all that happy, is she?" Hank countered.

It was obvious that he wanted to say something more, but he sensed it would only denigrate into really angry words that couldn't be taken back. He took a different tone.

"Look, I've got to go. Janie's in the truck, waiting for me," he said, his voice softening.

"I'll call you later in the week to let you know how she's doing," he told Anne.

She pressed her lips together to keep back a sob. She could feel it throbbing in her throat. "I love her, Hank."

"I know that," he answered. "And when she calms down, she'll know that, too. But it's going to take a while." Hank was almost at the front door before he doubled back to her. He paused only long enough to kiss the top of Anne's head and then tell her, "It'll be all right."

With that, he walked out.

Feeling as if he had ruined Annie's life for a second time, Danny did the only thing he could for her. He stayed away. He felt he needed to give her time to pick up the shattered pieces of her life and try to put them together again.

To keep busy, he threw himself into working on the ranch with a vengeance. Though he was asked, he refrained from telling Jamie anything that had happened on Halloween. He made a point of denying, whenever Jamie asked him, that anything was wrong.

Jamie knew better, but he bided his time

and rather than grilling him, he waited for his brother to volunteer the information on his own. Waited for him to explain why he was suddenly staying on the ranch 24/7 instead of going into town the way he had been doing.

Jamie strongly suspected that this changed behavior had something to do with Anne, but for now, he didn't prod. But it wasn't easy, watching Danny hurting, because he clearly was.

Danny didn't come back. Not that evening, not the following day, nor the day after that. He didn't come back and he didn't try to see her or get in touch with her in any way.

Had he just given up? Anne wondered. Or were those weeks they had spent together just a fluke? Did he really not care about her after all?

She'd been so sure, after they had made love on Halloween night, that they actually *were* meant to be together. But maybe those were just her hormones talking. Maybe she had talked herself into believing that he cared about her after all when he obviously didn't.

Because if he actually *did* care, then where was he? Why wasn't he calling, trying to get her to change her mind? Trying to find a way to help her convince Janie to move back in with her?

Anne continued to go to work at the clinic, continued doing everything that she had been doing, but she was only going through the motions. Inside, she felt as if she had been completely gutted. Her daughter hated her and the only man she had ever loved had abandoned her a second time after he had made her yearn for him.

She felt as if her life was going up in flames and there was absolutely nothing she could do about it.

But even so, she knew that somehow, she just had to.

Chapter 17

Anne's natural inclination was to hide. Not physically, but emotionally. To run and to reconstruct those walls that she had so diligently built up over the last twelve years.

The same walls that Danny had so effectively deconstructed like a velvet wrecking ball in one evening of unadulterated passion.

But she sensed that if she continued to do what she had always done, she could expect to get what she had gotten these last dozen years: a life of mind-numbing emptiness. Yes, she'd had Janie, but right now, she didn't even have her.

She knew that she needed to rethink her position as well as her situation. Did she *really* want to continue this way? To live her life without Danny because she wanted to protect Janie? To keep her daughter and herself from possibly being hurt?

In a perfect world, that might have been achievable. But this was far from a perfect world. It was a world where things sometimes got messy, despite the best of efforts and intentions.

Anne really wanted to win back her daughter and, just as important, she wanted to get Danny back in her life, even if that meant risking being vulnerable. Love was worth the risk and she loved Danny with all her heart.

Always had, always would.

It was about time that she grew up and acted like a woman, not like an adolescent, Anne silently upbraided herself.

Danny didn't know if it was the blazing sun that lit up the ranch as he worked next to his brother, but he was finally seeing things clearly. After a great deal of soul-searching he'd reached a conclusion. Leaving wasn't going to solve anything. It wasn't the answer to anything. Whether he was here or in Colorado, he was still Janie's father and now she knew it. What kind of a father would he be, running off again? Moreover, if he did that, just how would that make Janie feel?

Besides, he didn't want to leave. He really loved Annie. Halloween evening had just proved it to him. He loved Annie and if he left Rust Creek Falls, it would mean literally tearing himself apart.

The answer wasn't running back to Colorado or to any other state, even further away. The answer was to dig in and ride out whatever storm might come his way. Ride it out until the storm finally passed and the seas became calm.

Annie was worth anything he had to endure, as was Janie.

Danny sighed, leaning on the shovel he'd been using to dig postholes. But now that he had made up his mind to stay, just how did he go about getting from point A to point B? How did he get Annie to allow him back into her life?

That was the part he needed to figure out.

Next to him, Jamie dropped the sledgehammer he was wielding to pound the new replacement posts into the ground. The hammer hit the ground, falling to the side as he looked at his brother.

He and Danny had been at this, replacing fence posts, for over a day. For the most part, over the course of that time, the sound of the sledgehammer was the *only* sound that was heard. If not for that rhythmic noise, the silence surrounding the two of them would be close to deafening.

Danny realized that his brother had stopped working. "Something wrong?" he wanted to know, looking in Jamie's direction.

"Yes, something's wrong," Jamie answered, doing his best not to sound annoyed. "I've been a good brother and held my peace for as long as I could. I didn't push, I didn't pry, thinking that eventually, you'd open up that sealed tomb of yours that you call a mouth and finally *talk* to me.

"But you obviously like pretending you're a sphinx," Jamie complained, "so I'm going to break the silence for you and ask."

Danny looked at him, obviously confused. "Ask me what?"

Jamie bit back a curse. Instead, he just got

down to the bare bones of the question haunting him. "What the hell happened?"

"Happened?" Danny repeated as if he wasn't familiar with the word. It was clear that he was stalling, buying himself some time so he'd know how to frame his answer.

Jamie came dangerously close to losing his temper. "Damn it, Danny, you've never been an innocent, so don't try to play one now." Because Danny still wasn't talking, he went over the situation for him step by step. "You came home early Halloween night, dressed like a pirate and as silent as a crypt. Now, what the hell happened that night and why haven't you been to see Annie since then?

"Why have you suddenly become the epitome of a faithful hired hand, shadowing my every move like you don't have a mind of your own or anything else to do? Talk to me, damn it, or the next thing I'm liable to pound with that sledgehammer," he said as he nodded toward where it lay on the ground, "is your head."

Danny took a breath. Jamie was right. He couldn't keep this bottled up inside him any longer. He needed to talk, to get it off his chest so he could finally move forward. "We told her."

"Annie? Told her what?" Jamie asked, confused. "And who's 'we'?"

Dan shook his head. "No, not Annie. Janie. Annie and I told Janie that I'm her father."

"Her *what*?" Jamie cried, stunned. "Hold it, back up," he ordered. "*You're* Janie's father?" Dumbfounded, he stared at his brother. This was the first he'd heard of that. "Are you really sure about that?"

Dan nodded. "Annie told me. She didn't want me to say anything to anyone about it. I couldn't tell you," he began, ready with an apology that didn't make it past his lips.

Jamie waved his hand at his brother, silencing him. "I'm not mad that you didn't tell me. I'm just really surprised, that's all. Annie was away at college and when she finally came back, she was married to Hank. I just assumed that Janie was Hank's. The whole town assumed it."

"Well, she's not, and on Halloween night we told Janie I was her father and she didn't take it very well," he said sadly. "She accused us of lying to her and then she called Hank to come get her. She told Annie she was going to live with 'her father.' It tore Annie up right in front of my eyes. *I* did that to her," Dan said, the sadness audible in his voice.

There was nothing but sympathy in Jamie's eyes as he listened to his brother. "That's a lot for you to be carrying around."

"It's not me I'm thinking about. It's my fault this happened, because I came back," he said, feeling guilt sinking its teeth solidly into his conscience. "And now I have to find a way to fix this."

Jamie looked at him sharply. "Not by leaving again," he warned. "Even if I have to hogtie you, you are *not* going back to Colorado. You belong here. Not just for my sake or Bella's," Jamie told him, mentioning their sister. "Not even for my kids. You owe it to Annie and to Janie to stay."

Dan shook his head ruefully. "Janie hates me."

"Well, then you have to make her unhate you," Jamie said simply.

He was all for that. But there was just one little problem with Jamie's advice. "And how am I supposed to do that?"

"Go talk to her. Not like she's some little kid. Talk to her like she's an adult. Listen to your heart, Danny," Jamie advised. "The time comes, you'll know what to say to her."

"You've got a lot of faith in a guy you haven't seen in twelve years." Frankly he didn't know if he was up to it.

Jamie grinned at him. "Yeah, but don't forget, I've got a lot of memories to work with and I've got a good memory. No matter how rough the calluses are on your hands, you're still the same guy inside that was always there for me when we were growing up. That's what you tap into," Jamie told him. "Be there for her. Be there for your daughter."

And then he stopped as he looked at Danny, trying to absorb the impact of what he'd just been told. "Wow. You a father. Now, there's something that's going to take some getting used to," Jamie told him.

"No more than you being the father of triplets," Dan responded.

Jamie's eyes crinkled as he laughed. "I guess you've got a point." He stripped off his heavy-duty gloves and stuck them in his back pocket. "C'mon, I'll drive you back to the house. You've got to get cleaned up," he told his brother, adding, "You've got some fancy talking to do."

"What about work?" Danny asked, looking back at the posts that were still on the ground, waiting to be pounded in.

"Work's officially done for the day. Fallon's always after me to take an afternoon off. Looks like this is going to be it," he declared, getting in behind the steering wheel of his truck. "Now, are you going to get in, or are you planning on running alongside the truck until we get back to the house?"

"As appealing as that sounds," Danny said sarcastically, "I think I'll get into the truck." He slid onto the passenger seat.

When Danny looked back on it later, his return to Rust Creek Falls seemed to be fraught with giant bouts of nerves. Nerves had danced throughout his entire body when he'd first stood on Jamie's doorstep, waiting for his brother's first words to him.

The same complete uncertainty had telegraphed itself through his system when he'd stood before Annie's door, wondering what she would say when she finally saw him there.

And now he was going through the exact same thing as he waited for Hank to open his front door.

Dan counted off the seconds. Fifteen went by before the door finally opened. When it did, he found himself looking up at a less-than-friendly face. Hank was all but glaring at him.

"What do you want?" Hank demanded in a voice that was very close to a growl.

Dan silently congratulated himself that at least the other man hadn't slammed the door in his face. He took his victories where he found them.

"I'd like to talk to Janie," he answered.

Hank's eyebrows drew together in a dark, angry scowl. "Well, she doesn't want to talk to you."

Rather than turn around and leave, Dan made an appeal to the girl's stepfather. "Please, Hank. I need to explain some things to her."

Unmoved, Hank retorted, "You've already explained enough."

But Dan wasn't about to be dissuaded. "That's just it. I haven't. I need to make some things clear to her. And after I'm done, I'd like to talk to you, Hank," he said.

Hank looked skeptical, his eyes shrewdly assessing Dan. For a second, Dan thought

Janie's stepfather was going to turn him away. But then the rancher blew out an impatient breath and opened the door a little further.

"All right," Hank said. "Come in. But the first second Janie looks like she doesn't want to listen anymore, you're gone, even if I have to hurl you out the door myself. Understood?"

Dan nodded, relieved that Hank was giving him this chance. "Understood."

Resigned, looking far from happy about the situation, Hank turned and led the way into the large, sprawling living room.

Janie was on the sofa, watching TV. The second she saw Dan, she jumped to her feet. "What's *he* doing here?" she wanted to know, glaring angrily at the man next to Hank.

"He says he's here because he wants to talk to you," Hank told her.

"Do I have to?" Janie's voice bordered on whining as she stared defiantly at Dan.

"Hear him out, honey," Hank said, his voice taking on a kind tone when he spoke to the girl. "I raised you to be fair."

Janie sighed, put upon. "All right, if you want me to." She shifted her eyes in Danny's direction as Hank slipped into the background. "Go ahead," she said to Dan. "Talk."

Danny felt as if he was standing before a pint-size judge. Not exactly ideal conditions in his opinion, but they were the only ones he was going to get so he knew he had to make the most of them.

"I just wanted you to know that I didn't know you even existed until just a few weeks ago."

"Mom didn't tell you?" Janie demanded sharply.

He could see she was going to hold that against Annie, too, unless he talked quickly. "No. Your mother had no way to get in touch with me to let me know I had a daughter."

"Were you some kind of bad guy on the run?" Janie asked suspiciously.

"If you're asking me if I was a criminal, no, I wasn't a criminal," he told her. "But you could say that I was on the run." He saw his daughter looking at him quizzically but he didn't want to get into that just yet. "The important part is that your mother was trying to do what she thought was best for you and I don't want you to blame her for any of this, or to hold it against her, agreed?"

The frown on Janie's face told him that the girl wasn't capitulating, at least not yet. She was being defiant and he knew that he needed to convince her. He told her the only thing that he could. "I am never going to try to replace Hank.

"You're right, you know. Your 'real' dad is the one who was there for you, who raised you and encouraged you to do your best even when it wasn't easy. He got to spend the years with you that I couldn't, because I didn't know about you. I can never have that, just like I can never replace him.

"But I would very much like to get to know you, Janie, and get to spend some more time with you if you'll let me. And if you're willing to give me that chance, I think you'll get to see that I'm not really such a bad guy after all."

Dan looked at his daughter for a long moment, then put his hand out to her. "What do you say, Janie? Will you give me another chance?"

Janie frowned and chewed on her lower lip, debating whether or not to believe him. Still debating, she looked down at his hand. And then, finally, she slipped hers into it.

"I guess I can give you one more chance," she told him.

Dan felt as if his very insides had lit up like the candles on a birthday cake.

"I promise I won't disappoint you," he told his daughter, solemnly shaking the small hand.

"We'll see," Janie said, sounding every bit the way her mother did. "But I'm not going back to my mother," she warned.

"I understand. But I'd like you to think about it. She really misses you a lot and she really was trying to do her best for you. You have always been her first priority."

Janie shrugged, trying hard to sound distant. "We'll see."

"That's all anyone can ask," Dan told his daughter. "And it means a lot. To your mom and to me."

"Yeah," was all Janie would say, but from where he was standing, it sounded positive to Dan.

The first step had been taken, he thought. Now all he needed was to get Janie to keep walking.

Chapter 18

The moment it looked as if he and Janie had finished talking for now, Hank seemed to materialize out of the shadows and swooped in, looking extremely solemn.

"I'll see you out," Hank said.

It wasn't an offer. It was a command.

Dan felt like he was given his walking papers. Since he had said what he had come to say to Janie and the situation looked at least somewhat hopeful, he acquiesced to Hank's offer.

"Sure. See you, Janie."

The girl merely nodded, going back to her TV program.

Hank walked beside him in silence until they were at the front door again. Opening it, the stone-faced man surprised him by coming out with him to the front porch.

Once outside, Hank pulled the door closed behind him. It was obvious that the man wanted to talk, so Dan braced himself.

"I appreciate you not trying to strong-arm Janie into anything," Hank told him.

He'd had a feeling that Hank had been in the background somewhere, listening. It had made him doubly cautious as he'd chosen his words.

"I was serious when I said that all I wanted was a chance to get to know her," he told Hank.

Arms crossed before his chest, Hank stood studying him for a long moment, saying nothing. Dan had almost turned to leave when Hank finally said something further. And what he said *really* surprised him.

"You know she never got over you. Anne," Hank added, although there was no doubt who he was talking about. "I knew that when I married her. But I hoped that in time, she'd learn to love me. Not the way she loved you," he allowed, knowing that wasn't possible. "That kind of thing only comes along once in a lifetime. But there are other kinds of love," he said philosophically. "Gentle, patient kinds of love.

"But I learned that there was never going to be any room in Anne's heart for any other man but you. Eventually, I gave up trying to find a tiny space in that heart for me.

"I'm telling you this," Hank went on, "because if you're not sure about your feelings for her, you should leave now before you do any more damage to Anne—or to Janie. I won't stand for either one of them being hurt," Hank said adamantly. "They don't deserve it."

"No, they don't," Dan agreed quietly. "And I would die before I was the reason that either one of them wound up being hurt again."

"You did before," Hank pointed out. "You left Anne twelve years ago, vanishing out of her life without a single word."

He knew all that and the act weighed heavily on him now. "The circumstances were different back then."

"Anne was still Anne," Hank reminded him.

It wasn't that he wanted Hank not to blame him. He just felt that the rancher needed to understand why things had happened the way they had.

"And at the time I left, I felt that she deserved to be with someone who was better than me," Dan told him. The words seemed to be coming out of their own accord.

Hank frowned. "What's that supposed to mean?" he wanted to know. He couldn't help thinking that Dan was just attempting to snow him.

Okay, it was time, Dan decided. Time to let the other man know why he had left Rust Creek Falls and why he had stayed away as long as he had.

"It means that at the time I left, I really didn't feel worthy of anybody, least of all someone like Anne." Dan took a breath before he went on. The words hurt. There was no way of getting away from that. "I felt that I was responsible for my parents' deaths."

Hank looked at him, confused. "I heard that your parents died in a car accident."

"They did," Dan said grimly.

Dan blaming himself for something like that didn't make any sense to Hank. Unless... The thought struck him.

"Were you driving the car at the time?" Hank asked.

"No, but I was the reason that they *were* driving." Dan saw that Hank looked more confused than ever.

He hated this story, hated having to revisit it. But he felt that Hank needed to hear it so that the rancher could see Dan wasn't just some self-centered cowboy who came and went whenever the whim suited him without any thought to the people who mattered. Namely Annie and Janie.

Wishing he could shield himself somehow, knowing that just wasn't possible, Dan finally launched into the story that changed his life—and everyone else's.

"My two older brothers, Luke and Bailey, went out drinking one night. I went with them but at the time I didn't know that was what they intended to do. It wasn't too long before they were both much too drunk to drive home safely. I didn't have the keys to the car and Luke wouldn't give me his. I was afraid we'd all wind up in an accident—or worse— so I called my parents to ask them to come pick us up."

Hank shrugged, not hearing anything out

of the ordinary. "Sounds like a scene that happens every night all over the country," he acknowledged. "Parents come get their inebriated kids all the time."

"Except that those parents all get home in one piece," Dan said grimly. "Mine didn't." He looked at Hank. The rancher was obviously waiting to hear more. "Don't you see? If I hadn't called them to pick us up, my parents would still be alive."

Hank didn't quite see it that way. "Maybe yes, maybe no. When your time comes, you can't outrun your fate," the rancher said philosophically. And then he looked at Dan sharply. "Is this what you've been running from all this time?"

"Yes," Dan said heavily.

"A lot of things to feel guilty about in this world," Hank said. "Not being there for a good woman when she needed you is one. Not being there for your kid when she was growing up is another. But being responsible for your folks' deaths in a car accident when you weren't anywhere near that car? Get over yourself, Stockton," he told Dan. "You're not in charge of everything going on in the universe. Stuff happens and you're just another bystander."

And then he surprised Dan by putting his hand out to him in a show of tentative friendship.

Dan took it, finding himself on the receiving end of a hearty handshake.

"Thanks for trusting me with your story," Hank told him. "Now stop wasting time talking to me and go patch things up with Anne," he ordered.

Relieved, feeling as if a rock had been lifted from his shoulders, Dan murmured a heartfelt "Thanks" as he hurried off to his truck.

"Good luck," Hank called after him.

Dan acknowledged his words with a quick wave just before he got in behind the steering wheel.

The urgent knocking on her door startled Anne. Her first thought was that something had happened to Janie and someone was here to notify her.

Fairly running to the door, she threw it open and was startled to find Danny standing on her doorstep.

A wave of déjà vu passed over her, except that the first time, Danny's knocking hadn't been nearly so urgent as it was now.

She was about to ask what was wrong, but she never got the chance because the very next moment, Dan was scooping her up in his arms and then twirling her around, stealing her breath away, not to mention making her dizzy.

"No more running away," Danny declared, setting her down on her feet inside her house. He held her shoulders in an effort to keep her from losing her balance and falling over. "Even if you decide that you don't want us to be together, I want you to know that I'm not going anywhere anymore, and I'll be here any time you need me for any reason."

Annie looked at him uncertainly. "Then you're staying?"

"I'm staying," he confirmed. "I'm moving back to Rust Creek Falls permanently so I can get to really know our daughter—and be here for her, as well. I want to be a hands-on dad, not just one in name only."

She was afraid to believe him, but she had to admit, she was sorely tempted to. This what she'd been dreaming about all these years: Danny, coming back and wanting to take care of her and their daughter.

"And you're not going to change your mind tomorrow?" Anne asked.

"Not tomorrow, or the day after that, or the day after that times infinity," he replied. "I'm here to stay, Annie. Besides, where else would I go? The only woman I have ever loved lives here, so I can't go anywhere else."

He had never said those words out loud to her, even though she'd hoped and prayed that he would. "You love me?" she asked, wanting to hear him say it again.

"I love you," he repeated. "I loved you twelve years ago. I love you now and I will go on loving you until the day I die. Maybe a little longer than that," he added with a smile.

But Anne felt as if she needed a lot of assurance after what she'd been through. She was not about to begin building castles in the sky on a foundation of sand the way she had before.

"I can't help wondering if you're in love with me, or if you're just in love with the girl I used to be. The girl without a serious thought in her head," she recalled ruefully. Her eyes met his. "Because I'm not that girl anymore."

"I know that," Dan told her. "I know you're not the same person you were then. You've done a lot of growing and maturing over the years. You became a responsible mother and you were even willing to marry someone you weren't in love with just to give your daughter a stable life. And when you realized that you felt Hank deserved someone who loved him for himself, you divorced him even though doing that meant you had to make sacrifices in order to provide for your daughter. That's not something a girl 'without a serious thought in her head' would do. That's something a responsible woman would do," he told her.

"Twelve years ago," he went on, "I promised to protect you and stay by your side and I blew it. Right now, all I want to do is spend the rest of my life making it up to you—if you'll let me." He took her hands in his. "Will you?"

Anne stared at him, wondering if she understood him correctly.

"Are you saying what I think you're saying?" she asked, afraid to let herself believe that. What if she'd somehow misunderstood him? She didn't relish looking like a fool—or having her heart broken a second time.

Danny grinned. "I guess I'm not really any good at this," he confessed. "But in my defense, I've never proposed before."

"Proposed," Anne echoed, her eyes widening as she stared at the man in her living room.

"Proposed," Dan repeated with feeling. Taking her hands again and this time pressing them to his chest right over his heart, he said, "Anne Lattimore, I love you and I want to spend the rest of my life loving you. Will you marry me?"

He saw tears shining in her eyes, threatening to spill down her cheeks. "Tears," he said. "Are they good tears, or bad tears?"

Anne tried to answer, but her throat was completely choked with emotion and for a moment, she couldn't say a word.

Second guessing the reason for her silence, Dan wanted to put her mind at ease and told her, "Hank gave me his approval."

That surprised her.

"He what?" she cried, not really certain she liked the fact that her fate was being hashed out by the men in her life.

"He was trying to protect you, saying that if I wasn't completely committed to you—and to Janie—then I needed to go back to Colorado. That was when I explained to him why I left in the first place. He heard me out and then he came around."

She knew that sharing his reasons with Hank had to have been painful for Danny. "You did that?" she asked. "You told him what happened?"

"I would do anything if it meant that we could be together," he told Anne. "I went to talk to Janie about things. I got her to listen and I think she'll come around." All he wanted to do was show Anne how much he loved her.

And now that he had asked her to marry him, he wanted it to become a reality, but he felt he shouldn't rush her. Dan struggled to rein himself in.

"We don't have to set a date yet," he continued. "I just wanted you to know that I mean business because this time, I'm not planning on letting you get away—not ever again."

"You mean business," she repeated with a trace of amusement.

"Yes."

A wicked smile flirted with her lips. "Well, if you really mean business, then why don't you show me?"

"And how do you suggest I do that?" he asked her, bemused.

"You're a very smart man, Danny Stockton," she told him, lacing her arms around her neck. "I think you can figure it out."

"How many chances do I get?" he teased.

She could feel her heart accelerate as it swelled with joy. "As many as you need," she told him.

"Oh, good," he said just before he lowered his lips to hers. "Because I intend to use them all."

And he very nearly did.

Epilogue

"I can't believe that we've owned our old ranch this entire time and never realized it," Bella Stockton Jones said to her brothers in amazement.

She, Jamie and Dan moved around the first floor of the old house at Sunshine Farm, trying to avoid cobwebs as they wove their way through an incredible amount of dust and even more old memories.

"We still wouldn't have known about it if Zach Dalton hadn't come to me and asked if I would consider selling the old ranch to him," Jamie said, tugging back a drape and unleashing a swirl of dust.

"I told him I didn't know what he was talking about," Jamie continued. "That the ranch didn't belong to us. But Zach insisted that it did. He said that he'd looked it up in county records and according to them, the property was still ours."

"If it belonged to you, why didn't your grandparents tell you?" Annie asked, puzzled. She'd insisted on coming along for this walk-through in case Danny needed a little moral support for his return to his old family homestead.

"You're asking the wrong person," Dan told her. "I have no idea why those two old people did anything." He wasn't bitter toward his grandparents at this point—he was just sad.

"Maybe they felt too put-upon just taking care of us and didn't want to be bothered looking into anything else. They did take in two of us," Bella said, adding, "Grudgingly."

"Those days are best left behind us," Dan told his siblings. He had no desire to dig up any more painful memories. They had all had enough of those to last them a lifetime and a half and it was time to move forward.

"I guess we have a lot to thank the Daltons

for," Jamie said, crossing to the other end of the room and pulling back more drapes.

"You mean for telling us about the old Sunshine Farm?" Dan asked.

"That and airing that program of the triplets and me that Travis had documented. If it hadn't been for that—and for him—you would have never come back to Rust Creek Falls," Jamie pointed out.

Dan's hand tightened around Annie's. "Oh, I'd like to think that I would have come back eventually. But you're right," he agreed, looking at Jamie. "Travis was instrumental in making me finally decide that it was time to at least come back to see how everyone was doing."

"So now that you've taken a look around, what are you going to do with this place?" Anne asked, directing her question to all three Stocktons.

Jamie was the first to speak up. "I think we should try to fix it up." He looked at Dan and Bella. "What do you think?"

"Sounds good to me," Bella answered, nodding her head.

"I'm in," Dan told Jamie. "After helping you out at your place, I've gotten pretty good at fixing things up."

"I don't know about 'good.' I'd say that you're a work in progress at the moment," Jamie said with a laugh. "But sure, we could all pitch in to get this place looking livable again."

"Mom and Dad would have liked that," Bella told her brothers.

"Do you think you could have the ranch ready for a Christmastime wedding?" Anne asked quietly.

Dan whirled toward her. "Christmastime?" he repeated. "Is that when you want it?"

Her smile was almost shy as she answered, "Yes."

"Wait, hold it," Jamie spoke up, looking at Dan and Anne. "What wedding?"

"Are you two getting married?" Bella asked, excitement echoing in her voice before Dan could answer their brother's question.

"Yes. Yes, we are. And it looks like it's going to be a Christmas wedding," Dan said, pulling Annie close to him.

"Well, congratulations!" Jamie cried. "Let me be the first to kiss the bride-to-be."

"That's my job," Dan told him, elbowing Jamie out of the way. "You can be the second." With that, he kissed Annie. Under the circumstances, it was a quick kiss, but it expressed all the love he felt for her. "I just wish that the rest our siblings could be here for the wedding," he said wistfully.

"Don't worry," Jamie promised with determination. "They might not be here for the wedding, but we'll find them. I won't rest until we do."

"Neither will I," Bella added.

"That would be the very best wedding present of all," Anne told them, smiling up at Dan.

"See why I love her?" Dan asked his siblings. Looking at Annie, he said, "Yes, I totally agree, it would," just before he kissed her again.

It was the most happiness that the old homestead had seen in a decade—with more to come.

* * * * *

Get 4 FREE REWARDS!

We'll send you 2 FREE Books plus 2 FREE Mystery Gifts.

FREE Value Over **$20**

Both the **Romance** and **Suspense** collections feature compelling novels written by many of today's bestselling authors.

HARLEQUIN
PLUS

Announcing a **BRAND-NEW** multimedia subscription service for romance fans like you!

Read, Watch and Play.

Experience the easiest way to get the romance content you crave.

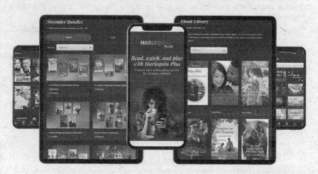

Start your **FREE 7 DAY TRIAL** at <u>www.harlequinplus.com/freetrial</u>.